PLOTS AND PLAYERS

I should like to thank the historian Dr Vivian D Lipman for allowing me to use his archive material about the Marrano community of Elizabethan London. I am also indebted to Lytton Strachey's biography of Elizabeth I for details of the Lopez conspiracy.

While the Fernandez family are fictitious, most of the other main characters—including the leaders of the Marrano community—are real people.

PLOTS AND PLAYERS

Pamela Melnikoff

Bedrick/Blackie
New York

For Edward

First published 1988 by Blackie and Son Ltd.
First American edition published in 1989
by Peter Bedrick Books, New York.

Library of Congress Cataloging-in-Publication Data.

Melnikoff, Pamela,
Plots and players/Pamela Melnikoff.
— 1st American ed.   p.   cm.
Summary: Robin, Philip, and Frances. exiled
Portuguese Jews secretly practicing their faith in
intolerant sixteenth-century London, fight against
the poison of prejudice in trying to save the life of
Queen Elizabeth's Jewish doctor.

ISBN 0-87226-406-8

[1. Jews—England—Fiction.
2. England—Social conditions—16th century— Fiction.
3. Prejudices—Fiction.]   I. Title.
PZ7.M5163P1   1989.

[Fic]—dc19.   88-13862
                                           CIP
                                           AC

10 9 8 8 7 6 5 4 3 2 1

Printed in Great Britain by
Thomson Litho Ltd, East Kilbride, Scotland

Chapter One

Robin was feeling nervous, and not just because it was Monday morning. All the boys in his class hated Mondays. On Sundays they were expected to go to church, and next day their teacher would test them on what they remembered of the sermon, and any boy who failed to please Master Breakstaff was likely to get a flogging. Mondays were always unpleasant, but today was a specially difficult day for Robin, because of his secret.

He sat stiffly on his bench, watching a yellow moth fluttering against the latticed panes, and wondering why the silly creature should want to beat its wings against the schoolroom window when it had the whole splendid city of London to fly about in. If *I* were a moth, he thought, I shouldn't be such a fool. His ruff prickled against his neck as if it were made of straw, and there was a dry feeling in his throat.

Master Breakstaff looked sternly around the classroom, his

face long and sharp as a weasel's behind its pointed beard. Then his eyes fell on Robin, and twenty other small boys breathed more easily.

'Robin Fernandez,' he said, and Robin felt his knees grow weak. Richard Lucy, his best friend, who sat next to him, nudged him happily.

'Now, Master Fernandez,' said the schoolmaster in his dry voice, 'let us see how much attention you paid to yesterday's sermon. We have not had the pleasure of hearing you discourse before. I suppose you *were* in church?'

'Yes, sir.'

'Very good. At what time did the preacher begin?'

'At seven o'clock.'

'And what was his text?'

'Proverbs, chapter three.'

'Excellent. So far, I must admit, you have done well. Now let us see if you remember what the venerable gentleman had to say. Begin.'

'Er . . . he . . . he was talking about wisdom. He said that . . . that our Lady the Queen rules this country well, not just because she was born to power, but because . . .'

'Because . . .?'

'Because she is wise.'

'And . . .'

Robin racked his brains desperately, but could not remember another thing – possibly because, though he *had* been in church, he had been playing marbles with his brother Philip in the back pew during the greater part of the sermon.

'Is that all?'

Robin dropped his eyes, partly in shame, and partly so as not to see the birch rod that hung menacingly on the wall behind Master Breakstaff's head.

'You remember nothing more?'

'No, sir.'

'And are you proud of your achievement?'

6

Robin admitted that he was not.

Master Breakstaff eyed the birch rod thoughtfully for a few moments, and then smiled a frosty smile.

'Very well. I do not fear that *your* wisdom will ever bring you power, Master Fernandez. I shall not punish you this time, because you are a newcomer to our school and our city, but I could not say with any truth that Bristol's loss has been London's gain.'

The other boys giggled dutifully, and Robin blushed and promised to do better in future.

'He let you off lightly,' said Richard Lucy later that morning as the boys – accompanied by Philip, who was in a lower class – set off home for their dinner. 'He knows that people who come from Bristol can't help being stupid.'

Arguing over the rival merits of their birthplaces was a favourite pastime with Richard and Robin. The Fernandez family had moved from Bristol only a few weeks earlier to settle in the London parish of St Olave's, Hart Street. But today Robin felt too worried to join in the usual game of 'My city is better than yours'. Today it was enough that he was a Marrano, a secret Jew, practising his religion behind locked doors, always fearful of discovery and death . . . and that this was the eve of Passover.

Yet his thoughts must not seem to wander, or Richard, his best friend, might grow suspicious.

'Bristol folk are *not* stupid,' he protested, as the boys emerged into Paul's Churchyard. 'We have a public library, which is more than you have in London.'

'A public library? Who needs public libraries when we have so many booksellers? *Our* citizens *buy* books, and pay good money for them.' And Richard waved a triumphant hand towards Paul's Churchyard, which was crammed with bookshops and bookstalls. In front of each dark shop door-way, below the gaily-painted sign that swung and creaked in the breeze, stood a trestle-table where scholarly tomes and

7

gold-bound volumes of poetry and philosophy, magic and romance rubbed covers with maps, pamphlets, bawdy ballads and lurid accounts of public executions. All kinds of folk jostled and clamoured round the stalls, thumbing through the volumes or guffawing over the ballads . . . venerable gentlemen in flat caps and fur-trimmed robes; scholars in shabby gowns; countrymen up for a day in town; the occasional gallant, bright as a peacock in his velvet cloak and embroidered doublet, with a jewelled sword glittering at his hip.

> 'O Bristol is a fine city,
> And so begins my little ditty,'

sang Richard as the boys went on their way towards Cheapside.

> 'O Bristol is a fine city;
> It stands upon a hill,
> And if I had not left it,
> Then I should dwell there still.'

He pretended to strum the lute as he sang, making Robin giggle in spite of himself.

And now Cheapside lay before them, with all its glorious noise and spectacle. The boys did not really need to go through Cheapside in order to reach St Olave's, but they preferred to take this longer way home. It was worth missing a little of their precious dinner-break to glimpse the splendid, tall houses of Goldsmith's Row, and the shops full of gold and silver plate, and the market where all the goods in the world were on sale, from lace, ribbons, ruffs and trinkets to beard-brushes and toothpicks, sweetmeats and hot pies. Half the citizens of London seemed to be crowding round the stalls, and the melodious cries of the traders, cries of 'What d'ye lack, my masters?' and 'New brooms, green brooms!' rose high above the chatter of their customers. Every so often a porter staggered past, bent almost double under some heavy burden, or a chimney-sweep, black as his own brush, or a coach or cart came clattering over the paving-stones, spattering mud over someone's silk stockings or satin petticoat.

'I've a penny that my uncle gave me,' announced Richard as the boys came to a stall that sold tempting-looking cakes. 'Shall we have almond tarts or quince pie?'

Robin's heart sank. Passover had already begun, and as practising Jews he and Philip were forbidden for the next eight days to eat any food made with flour.

'Buy whatever you like,' he said hastily. 'We're not allowed to eat cake.'

'*What*?'

'Er . . . we have the stomach-ache.'

Richard stared at the brothers. 'What, *both* of you?'

They nodded miserably.

'What delicate creatures you Bristol fellows are!' Richard went on. 'You never eat meat . . .'

'That's because we have the black bile,' said Robin hastily.

'And you never touch oysters, or eel pie . . .'

'That's because we suffer from the gout in our family.'

'Then what do you live on? Lettuce?'

'We don't go hungry,' murmured Robin, watching enviously as Richard bought his almond tarts and began to munch with relish.

'Well, go home to your miserable dinner and I'll go to mine,' cried Richard, as the boys parted company. 'Our cook has been making pork pies all morning.'

He ran off cheerfully, brushing the crumbs from his mouth with his sleeve, and left Robin and Philip to trudge on dolefully towards St Olave's.

The house was in turmoil when they arrived home. It had been cleaned from top to bottom in preparation for Passover,

9

and now the servants were busy strewing fresh rushes and sprinkling sweet-smelling herbs over the floors. All the gilt and silver plate had been polished; the hangings and tapestries, tablecloths and napkins laundered, and the rooms decorated with flowers and leafy branches. Special cooking-pots, dishes, goblets and table utensils that usually lay hidden in a secret chest had been brought out to replace those used throughout the year. For Passover commemorated the Exodus from Egypt of the ancient Israelites, who had departed from slavery in such a hurry that there had been no time to leaven their bread. The festival lasted for eight days, and during that time Jews were not allowed to eat any food that contained leaven, or even to use the utensils that had come in contact with such food. On the previous evening the children, having first gone out of their way to eat up all the left-over cakes, accompanied Father as he moved round the house with a lighted candle, searching for any crumbs of leavened food that might be lurking in nooks and crannies. These had been swept up with a feather and ceremoniously burned. Now in the kitchen piles of newly-baked matzot – the cakes of unleavened bread that were eaten instead of ordinary bread during Passover – were being taken out of the huge oven; fish and fruit were stewing in giant cauldrons, and the maids were cleaning vegetables and preparing sides of beef and lamb and a great heap of chickens, geese and ducks for the spits.

Mother, who was supervising the cooking, turned to smile at the boys as they put their heads round the kitchen door.

'It's no use staring and sniffing,' she said. 'You've only boiled mutton and turnips for your dinner now, but you shall have a great feast tonight, God willing. We're expecting important guests to the Seder, and we have to make a good impression.' The boys already knew that the Mendes family were coming to the Seder. Ruy Mendes was a wealthy merchant who imported perfumes and spices from the East, and Father had recently gone into partnership with him. That was why the Fernandez family had moved from Bristol to London.

When Robin and Philip went into the small dining parlour for their dinner, they found their sister Frances already there, eating her boiled mutton but without much appetite. She looked pale, and her eyes were red.

'Something awful happened today,' she said, as the boys sat down beside her. 'Mother called me into her bedchamber this morning after you left for school, and she gave me some terrible news.' Here Frances sniffed miserably, and balanced a fragment of turnip on the end of her knife.

'Terrible news?' said Robin in alarm. 'Has someone found out about us being secret Jews?'

'I shouldn't care if they did. I'm so wretched that I shouldn't mind being deported. Or killed, even. You know that the Mendes family are coming to us for the Seder tonight?'

'Yes.'

'Well, Mother told me that they're bringing my husband with them.'

'But you haven't got a husband,' said Philip, staring at her in surprise.

'Not yet, silly, but I *shall* have. Mother told me today that Father had made a match between me and the Mendes's older son, Thomas. Mother said I would soon be old enough to be married and mistress of my own home.'

'I suppose so,' said Robin thoughtfully. Frances was eleven, a year younger than him and two years older than Philip.

'I don't see what's so terrible about getting married,' said Philip. 'Won't you enjoy having your own household, and servants to order about?'

'Oh yes . . . if only I could have *them* without having a husband. Suppose I don't like him? Suppose he doesn't like

11

me? Tell me, you've met the Mendes boys in synagogue, haven't you? What are they like?'

Robin looked at his sister's anxious face and pleading eyes, and he felt a sudden urge to tease her.

'Which one is Thomas?' he asked solemnly. 'Is he the short one with a squint, or the fat one with a hump?'

Frances stared at him in horror.

'Don't take any notice of him,' said Philip, trying hard not to laugh. '*I've* seen them, and they don't have squints or humps. At least, I don't think they do. Mind you, they're not exactly handsome. And I thought they looked rather dull.'

Frances sighed.

'There's only one good thing about all this awful business,' she said. 'Mother says I'm to have some new dresses made for my betrothal, and I may choose what I like. I shall have a wheel farthingale, in red velvet, and another with pearls on it, *and* silk stockings, *and* a three-piled ruff, *and* a yellow satin petticoat. Satin is very dear – twelve shillings a yard – but I don't care. If I have to marry Thomas Mendes, I don't see why I shouldn't have a yellow satin petticoat.'

'You're quite right,' said Robin. 'I'm glad *I* don't have to marry him.'

As soon as dinner was over the boys hurried back to afternoon school. Mother came to the door to see them off.

'Come home this evening as quick as you can,' she said. 'No playing leapfrog in the gutter, please, or dawdling in Cheapside. You have to go to synagogue before the Seder, and I don't want you to be late.'

'I wish we could stay at home for Passover,' said Philip in pleading tones.

Mother smiled sadly.

'One day, perhaps, we may be able to celebrate our festivals as they should be celebrated,' she said. 'But, for the

12

time being, no one must know. It is not so long since your grandparents died at the stake for being Jews.'

The boys shivered, and did not argue. any more. Suddenly the warm Spring air felt very cold.

The Marranos who lived in England had come as refugees from persecution in Spain and Portugal. Most of the Jews had been expelled from those countries a century ago, but many had remained, pretending to convert to Catholicism, though they still practised their faith in secret. But the spies of the Inquisition had tracked them down. Some of the secret Jews had been tortured and then burned at the stake; the rest had escaped and found new homes in England, Holland and Belgium.

The Fernandez family had come from Portugal to settle in England twenty years earlier, and the three Fernandez children never grew tired of listening to their parents' tales of that distant land where oranges and pomegranates grew and the sun burned as fiercely as the heretics' funeral pyres. They shivered as they listened, aware that they were still not safe. Somewhere a spy might be lurking, a chance word would betray them . . . and then they would be expelled from Queen Elizabeth's kind and tolerant land and shipped back to Portugal – and the arms of the Grand Inquisitor.

'Of course most of our friends and neighbours know that we Portuguese are Jews by birth,' Father explained. 'What they do *not* know is that we still observe our Jewish rites in secret. We are not persecuted for being Jews . . . it is no crime to be born a Jew, provided one embraces Christianity. It is only a crime to practise the Jewish religion.'

'But why? We don't do anything wicked.' Father smiled sadly.

'If I could answer that,' he replied, 'then I should be wiser than Solomon.'

* * *

13

In school that afternoon there was no opportunity to forget Mother's warning. The lessons included readings from the Scriptures, and because Easter was coming the children were told how the 'infidel Jews' had called for Jesus to be crucified. Robin and Philip, blushing in silence, had heard the Jews described as 'Christ-killers' many times before, and like those other teachers in Bristol, Master Breakstaff did not remind his pupils that Jesus, Mary and all the disciples had also been Jews.

But this time there was worse to come. When Master Breakstaff, about to complete the Scripture lesson, asked if any pupil had a question, a boy jumped to his feet.

'Sir,' he cried, 'what does ritual murder mean?'

'Ritual murder? By the Jews?'

'Yes, sir. There was a monk, a holy father, down by the river when I went home for dinner. There was a crowd about him, and he was warning them to keep their children safe indoors. He said the Jews always steal a Christian child at this time of the year, and crucify him, and mix his blood into their unleavened bread. Sir, is it true?'

Master Breakstaff stroked his beard.

'I have heard this story many times,' he said, 'and I believe it to be true. If the Jews were capable of killing our Lord, they must surely be capable of killing Christian children. So you had better hurry home tonight without dawdling, Master Lambert, or you may end your days as a saint and martyr rather than the idle, useless boy that you are.'

As the other boys giggled uneasily, Robin felt his own blood run cold. It's a wicked lie, he thought. We never kill anybody. Besides, we're not allowed blood in our food. We even have to soak and salt our meat before it's cooked, to get rid of the blood . . . But he had to remain silent, clenching his fists in anger, as Master Breakstaff told his pupils about Little St Hugh, who – so it was said – had been killed by the

14

Jews, and whose bejewelled tomb in Lincoln Cathedral had been revered by generations of Christian pilgrims.

When Robin and Philip arrived home they told Father what Master Breakstaff had said, and he looked grave.

'So they're putting that foul lie about again, are they?' he said. 'I thought we had heard the last of it. Yes, I know the story of Little St Hugh of Lincoln. His body was found in a well in a Jew's house in the year 1255. It turned out later that he had been killed by a tramp, but a hundred Jews were arrested on a blood ritual charge. Several were hanged without trial, but some good monks pleaded for the rest, and they were set free . . .'

'Good monks?' cried Philip, much surprised. '*Are* there good monks?'

'Of course. There are good men of every faith. But not enough of them, alas. Not enough. In Portugal, now, Passover was always a time of special terror for the Jews.'

'Why Passover?' asked Robin, curiosity overcoming fear.

'Because our enemies always chose the time of our release from bondage to remind us that we were still slaves. One Seder night, a hundred years ago, all the Jewish children in Portugal were forcibly baptized. Another time, thousands of New Christians were massacred in the streets after being caught celebrating the Seder in secret.' Father paused, looked at the boys' horrified faces, and then smiled. 'But enough of sad things! We have a feast coming. Go and change into your best clothes, and try to remember to wash your ears.'

When the Fernandez children, scrubbed clean and combed and dressed in all their finery, peered round the door into the great hall that evening, the long table was laid ready for the Seder ceremonials. There were cushions on all the chairs, so that the guests could recline as free men, not as slaves. A pile of matzot nestled under an embroidered silk cover. The Hagadah, a book containing the order of service, lay at each place. A large platter bore mementos of that night, long ago, when the Israelites had left Egypt. A cup of salt water recalled their tears, and grated horseradish the bitterness of their existence. A paste made of grated nuts, apples, cinnamon and wine represented the mortar that had fastened the bricks of Pharaoh's treasure-cities. Vegetables reminded the company of God's bounty; a roasted egg symbolized mourning and rebirth. And the shankbone of a roast lamb stood for the Paschal lamb whose blood, daubed on the doorposts, had instructed the Angel of Death to pass without stopping over the Israelite rooftops.

Soon the company, seated round the table, would hear Philip, as the youngest child present, ask why this night was different from all other nights. Father would reply, 'Once we were slaves in Egypt, but God brought us forth with a mighty hand and an outstretched arm . . .' The guests would nibble the matzot, and taste the various strange items, and sip four cups of wine, scattering drops in memory of the ten plagues God had visited on the Egyptians. There would be a fine meal, and prayers- and psalms of thanksgiving, and riddles, and discussions, and wonderful songs.

Already the sun was setting, and when the sky deepened to red Passover would begin. Mother would light the candles, and Father would recite the blessing with which Jews introduced all religious festivals, happy or sad: 'Blessed art Thou, O Lord our God, King of the Universe, who hast kept us in life, and preserved us, and enabled us to reach this season.'

The Mendes family arrived at the Fernandez house in great style that evening. Master Ruy Mendes, a large, portly gentleman with a red face that matched his velvet gown, had a gold neck-chain that must have weighed five pounds, and Mistress Mendes wore a bejewelled three-piled ruff . . . the kind Frances yearned for and Mother called extravagant.

The two Mendes boys stood meek and silent in the shadow

16

of their splendid parents. Thomas was a tall boy of fifteen, rather pale and solemn, in a black velvet doublet. His younger brother, Henry, was small and puny for his eleven years . . . But no one paid any attention to him anyway.

The most dangerous part of the evening, Robin knew, would be that moment in the service when the door opened to admit the prophet Elijah, protector of the Jewish people. He was said to visit each Jewish home during the Seder to sip the goblet of wine specially set aside for him. No one ever saw him, but all were aware of his presence. It was at this moment that any spy lurking outside the door to entrap the secret Jews could break into the house and catch them amid all their guilty ceremonials. Then there would be no Seder the following year, or ever again.

When the time came, it was Robin who was sent to open the door. His heart was thumping hard as he turned the heavy key and lifted the latch. The entire company had risen to their feet, and now lifted their wine goblets in greeting. Silent and invisible, Elijah entered the house, accompanied by a draught of cold air that made the guests shiver. Robin searched the shadowy doorway for signs of an intruder, and then glanced fearfully along the street. Except for a chink of light from the occasional shutter all was dark and peaceful under the moon.

When Robin returned to the dining-hall, having carefully locked and bolted the door again, Father and Master Mendes were discussing the Exodus as if it had happened yesterday and not four thousand years ago. 'That was all in the past,' Robin wanted to cry. 'What about our present sufferings? What about my grandparents, who were tortured to death for no worse a crime than observing their religion? What about us, in danger every hour of the day?' He did not even realize he had spoken aloud till he saw all the company looking at him in surprise. Even Thomas had stopped nibbling almonds and was staring at him open-mouthed.

'We have been persecuted in every generation,' Father replied at last, 'and yet, for all that, we are commanded never to forget how God brought us out of bondage long ago.'

'But when will we stop being persecuted?' Robin protested. 'When shall we be allowed to practise our religion openly?'

'Practise our religion openly?' Master Mendes laughed uproariously. 'Live openly as Jews? My dear boy, men will fly to the moon first.'

Robin did not reply. It seemed there was no answer to his question. Soon the evening ended, and the Mendes family took their leave, after inviting the Fernandez family to the Seder at their house the following night.

Later that night, looking from his bedroom window, Robin could just make out the pinnacles of the City wall as it snaked along behind the houses. On one side of the wall lay the leafy silence and darkness of the countryside, the hushed fields stretching away to the villages of Stepney and Stratford Bow. On the other side the sharp, pointed roofs and crowded steeples of London clustered against the clear sky, pierced at intervals by the glow of a lantern or a spark of candlelight. Behind the friendly rooftops lay the sinister slit-eyed turrets of the Tower, and beyond that, the gleaming river. Robin heard the distant voice of the watchman crying:

'Give ear to the clock, beware your lock,
Your fire and your light, and God give you goodnight,
Twelve o'clock!'

Then chime after chime of bells began to ring out from the City churches till the night was alive with them.

What had Master Mendes said? 'Live openly as Jews? Men will fly to the moon first.' The moon shone as bright as silver in the sky, and so did the stars, but Robin could see no trace of any flying men.

Chapter Two

There was a visitor in school next morning. He arrived in the middle of choir practice, and stayed to hear the boys sing their madrigals.

The newcomer was a young man with a high, balding forehead and merry brown eyes. Robin knew who he was, though he had not met him in the schoolroom before. He and Richard Lucy had once seen him coming out of a tavern with a crowd of friends – all of them talking and laughing, with manuscripts under their arms – and Richard had pointed him out to Robin and said proudly, 'That's Will Shakespeare . . . he writes plays for the Lord Chamberlain's Men, and he's an actor, too. He writes the best plays to be seen anywhere in London. I've seen some of them, and I've sung in them as well. I sang a solo in the last one – it was called *The Two Gentlemen of Verona*.'

Robin knew this to be true, even though it sounded

suspiciously like boasting. His school made a special study of music and singing; its choristers were often chosen to appear in plays and Court revels, and Richard could sing like a lark.

And now here was Will Shakespeare in person, come to choose some choristers for his next play. He listened attentively as the boys sang.

'Master Lucy, I shall want you as a soloist again,' he said when the song came to an end, and Robin looked at Richard enviously. I've quite a good voice too, he thought, and I've a solo part in the next song. If I do well, he might choose me too. The idea was so exciting that he swallowed too hard and nearly choked. Luckily he recovered in time to sing his piece as beautifully as he could.

Master Shakespeare looked impressed. 'You have a good voice, boy,' he said. 'I have not seen you before. What is your name?'

'Robin Fernandez, sir.'

'Fernandez? Then you are not English?'

'I was born in Bristol but my parents are Portuguese, sir,' replied Robin, his voice trembling a little, a sudden fear gripping his insides. 'Of course, our friends and neighbours know that we Portuguese are Jews by birth,' Father had told him. Would Master Shakespeare guess that his new discovery was a Jew? A practising one, perhaps?

But the playwright smiled, his eyes warm and friendly.

'So it is your Southern blood that gives you that olive complexion and those dark eyes. My dear Robin, I have been searching all over London for a boy with your colouring, but all the singing boys I can find are little blue-eyed English lads. Very pretty, of course, but I want a dark lad to play Rosaline . . .'

All the boys stared at Robin, and it was Richard's turn to look envious.

'This is not a speaking part,' Will Shakespeare went on, 'but it needs to be well played. Ah, but I have not yet told

20

you anything about the play . . . It is called *Romeo and Juliet*, and it is set in Italy. This Rosaline is a dark, fiery girl who torments her lover by pretending to ignore him. Now, in this scene, Rosaline and Romeo are both attending a masked ball. He gives her pleading looks, but she sweeps past him with her nose in the air and addresses all her smiles and friendly words to other men. Later, when she sees Romeo paying court to Juliet, she regrets her coldness and begins to feel jealous. But by then it is too late. It is *his* turn to ignore *her* . . .' Master Shakespeare broke off, looked at Robin's eager face, and smiled kindly. 'Now, could you do that, my boy?'

Robin nodded, too overcome to speak.

'Well, let me see you try. I shall play Romeo. Come now . . . sweep past me, and look haughty. And try to walk gracefully, like a woman . . . Remember, you will be wearing a skirt on stage, not breeches. You moved just now as if you were about to jump over a gate.'

Robin obligingly slowed down and began to take little mincing steps. He knew that all the other boys were watching him, and at first this made him nervous. But soon he forgot his audience, and even himself, as the character of Rosaline seemed to take hold of him. It was strange . . . all at once he *was* this proud Italian girl moving in a cloud of silks and velvets to the stately music of the dance, and when Romeo looked at him pleadingly he turned away with a taunting smile and a graceful toss of his head. He acted out the rest of the scene without effort, moving easily from coyness to jealousy and regret. It was very strange . . . Robin himself could not understand it. He had never been inside a theatre, and yet he had always felt this wild excitement at the sight of a playbill pasted on a wall. It was as if this moment had been waiting for him all his life . . . The boys suddenly broke into applause, and Robin stared at them, wondering for a moment where he was and what had happened to him.

21

Master Shakespeare was also clapping, his eyes alight with pleasure.

'Why, the boy is a born actor,' he cried. 'Have you ever played on a stage before, Robin?'

'No, sir,' said Robin, blinking a little.

'Well, you are what we call a "natural". With a little training you could be a fine actor. Would you *like* to come into the theatre?'

'Oh yes, sir,' gasped Robin, his eyes full of glorious visions.

'Well, you must ask your father first . . . I'll not be accused of kidnapping. Then, if he agrees, you can be apprenticed to our company as soon as you leave school. I can't take you as an apprentice myself, seeing that I have no wife to care for you, but Master Burbage or Master Heminges will be able to find a place for you, I dare say. In the meantime, rehearsals for *Romeo and Juliet* begin next Monday at the Rose Theatre in Southwark. I am pleased with this morning's work. Robin, if you do well as Rosaline I may even write a few lines for you.' And with this promise, and a warm smile, Will Shakespeare took his leave.

When he had gone, the other boys milled about Robin in excitement. Richard Lucy was among them, trying – though not too hard – to disguise his envy.

'This is better than Bristol, isn't it?' he said, clapping Robin on the back. 'You've no proper playhouse there, and no Will Shakespeare either.'

And Robin, smiling happily, did not even bother to argue.

Father was not quite so happy when he heard the news that evening.

'I'll have no son of mine earning his living in the theatre,' he said firmly, 'so you must forget any crazy notions that Master Will Shakespeare may have put into your head.' He was dressing for the Seder at the Mendes house; his thick gold chain flashed as he placed it round his neck, but Robin could see nothing but a bright blur through the tears of disappointment in his eyes.

'But, Father,' he said, his voice trembling, 'Master Shakespeare said I had a natural talent for the theatre.'

'Of course. He would insist that you had a natural talent for digging ditches if he wanted a ditch dug. Surely you know you are to be apprenticed to the Grocers' Guild so that you may come into our family business when you are older. Become an actor, indeed! Medicine and commerce are the only fit professions for a Jew . . . the theatre is for heathens.'

'But, Father . . .'

'Yes, it is true that I send you to a school that teaches music and singing, but that is because I intend you to become a lay cantor of our synagogue. I would have you employ the voice God has given you in the service of our community . . . not squander it on a pack of noisy groundlings who swear and shout and spit orange pips all over the stage. As for the actors, they are nothing but tinselled vagabonds. You have never been inside a theatre, have you?'

Robin admitted that he had not.

'Well, I once allowed myself to be taken to the theatre in Bristol for my sins, and it's no place for a well-brought-up Jewish boy, believe me.' Father looked at Robin's sad face, and his voice grew gentler. 'I've no wish to deprive you of your pleasure altogether, so you may take part in this play as a chorister. But I'll not have you dressing up in a skirt and playing a woman . . . it is forbidden by Jewish law. A chorister, but nothing more. You may tell Master Shakespeare that.'

And with this crumb of comfort, Robin had to be content.

When the family arrived at the Mendes house for the Seder, Robin soon forgot his disappointment.

The house, as Father had promised, was a splendid one,

with a great dining-hall and a long gallery full of family portraits. But it was the company that Robin found most exciting.

There was Dunstan Ames, leader of the Marrano community, a wealthy merchant who supplied the Queen's Household with its groceries; Dr Hector Nunez, who, it was rumoured, fed the Queen's ministers with secret information from Spain and Portugal and had even been able to warn them of the coming of the Armada. And then there was Dr Rodrigo Lopez, son-in-law of Dunstan Ames, and physician-in-chief to the Queen. He must surely be the most powerful man in England, thought Robin, for only he could give orders to Her Majesty and know that they would be obeyed. He could send her to bed when she was ill; he could command her to rest when she had been working too hard; he could give her nasty medicine to take, and even stand over her while she swallowed it. And yet he seemed quite ordinary, and not in the least powerful, as he sat at Master Mendes's Seder table, a little old man in a simple furred gown and gold chain – no different from the clothes Father wore – and looking frail and a little tired as he lifted the first cup of wine to his lips.

When the main part of the service was over, and the meal had been served, Robin pricked up his ears, trying as hard as he could to listen to the adults' conversation. It was not easy, for Philip, who sat next to him, was talking about a flogging he had received in school that day, while Frances, sitting facing him, was trying to coax a few words out of Thomas . . . all in vain, for he sat munching silently and ignoring her.

'I didn't really deserve a beating – it is just that I got my Latin verbs wrong . . .'

'Do you like my dress, Thomas? I'm going to have a yellow satin petticoat . . . just wait till you see it.'

Robin, longing to yell at them both to be quiet, strained

his ears towards the end of the table, where he could just make out fragments of what seemed like a most exciting conversation. The adults, as far as he could tell, were discussing someone called Dom Antonio, who it seemed was a claimant to the throne of Portugal. He was living in poverty somewhere in England, and some of his followers were actually lodging in Dr Lopez's house. More than that, Dr Lopez appeared to be plotting, together with the Earl of Essex, to restore Don Antonio to his throne. Robin trembled with joy at the thought of actually being in the same room as people who talked so casually about thrones and noblemen, plots and pretenders.

'I didn't get *all* my Latin verbs wrong – just some of them,' Philip droned on relentlessly in Robin's ear.

'Do you like dancing, Thomas?' asked Frances, as the gloomy Thomas stopped eating and began to lecture her on the evils of frivolity.

Oh, be quiet! Robin wanted to cry, for Dr Lopez had gone on to talk about the great Earl of Essex, the Queen's favourite, and his own dearest friend, and Robin hated to miss a single word.

So Richard Lucy was right, he thought, and London *was* the greatest city in the world. Where in Bristol could a boy like himself come so close to Court matters and affairs of State, or sit at table with a man who actually gave medicine to the Queen? London was like a casket full of rare jewels . . . and yet it was a dangerous place too. In Bristol a secret Jew could hide himself, but London was thick with spies and intrigues. Yes, life might be more vivid in London, but death was always closer.

It was at this point that Dr Lopez stopped talking about his friends at Court, and smiled at the children. His eyes, Robin noticed, were very dark and bright.

'And how are my young friends?' he asked kindly. 'We have heard nothing from you all evening. Thomas, my boy, your father tells me you are betrothed. Are you looking forward to marrying this lovely young lady?'

'Sir, my father says I must, and I always obey my father,' replied Thomas solemnly. All the adults laughed at this; Thomas looked surprised, and Frances looked furious.

'Spoken like a true gallant,' chuckled Dr Lopez. 'I hope you are writing poems in praise of her beauty.'

'I wrote her a Latin oration,' said Thomas. 'It was a translation of King Solomon's verses on a woman of virtue. My schoolmaster checked the grammar for me, and I didn't make a single mistake.' Here Thomas looked triumphantly at Philip, who retaliated by kicking his shins under the table.

'My boys have always loved scholarship,' said Master Mendes proudly. 'They would rather have a Latin verse than a sweetmeat.' The Fernandez children, who had been watching Thomas guzzling sweetmeats all evening, looked at each other and smiled nastily.

Their own father – feeling that his family was being overlooked – now broke into the conversation.

'My boy Robin received a great honour this morning,' he said proudly, and Robin stared at him in astonishment. 'A certain Master Shakespeare, whom I believe to be a playwright, visited his school, and chose him for a part in his next play. He declared that Robin sings beautifully and is a born actor.'

'Will Shakespeare?' exclaimed Dr Lopez eagerly. 'Why, he is a most gifted writer . . . a young man, but the Queen thinks highly of him. And he belongs to a fine company, the Lord Chamberlain's Men. If *he* has chosen your son for a part, then the boy must indeed be talented.'

'Of course he is talented . . . all my children are talented, in their own ways,' replied Father with a sly glance at Master Mendes. 'But naturally I cannot allow him to accept Master Shakespeare's offer. The theatre is no place for a Jewish boy.

26

I have told him that he may appear in this play as a chorister, but no more.'

'Oh, that would be a pity,' said Dr Lopez, and Robin's heart leaped in sudden hope. 'I see no harm in a little play-acting, Master Fernandez. Why, I used to take part in private theatricals myself, as a young man . . .'

'But this is a public theatre,' interrupted Master Mendes, 'and I agree with my good friend that play-acting is no fit profession for a Jewish boy.'

'Who talks of professions?' replied Dr Lopez. 'If *I* could combine theatricals with medicine, then why cannot young Robin combine theatricals with soap and spices? Let him take this one part, Master Fernandez, seeing that Will Shakespeare has offered it to him . . . but make it clear that the boy is not going to make acting his livelihood.'

Robin wanted to rush to the head of the table and hug Dr Lopez, but, being well brought up, he looked down meekly at his plate and said nothing.

'You may be right, Dr Lopez,' said Father, pleasantly aware that Master Mendes was turning green with envy. 'It *does* seem a pity that true talent should be thwarted.'

Dr Lopez smiled at Robin in a friendly way. 'So you sing and act well enough to please Master Shakespeare,' he said. 'And are you equally skilled on the strings? Which instrument do you play best?'

'The lute, sir.'

'And do you compose at all?'

'A little, sir.'

'Good. I should like to hear your music. Why not have supper with me at my house tomorrow night? And your brother and sister too, of course. Bring your lute, and your own songs. Your father will tell you where I live.'

'I . . . I . . . thank you, sir,' stammered Robin, too overcome to say any more.

27

'We shall expect you, then, with your parents' permission. At six o'clock.'

The rest of the night passed like a dream for Robin. It was only later, as he tossed and turned in the great four-poster bed, too excited to sleep, that he remembered that Thomas Mendes and his younger brother Henry had not been included in Dr Lopez's invitation to supper.

Chapter Three

Dr Lopez lived just outside London in a fine house in Holborn, a quiet place surrounded by green fields and gardens yet only a stone's throw from the hubbub of Cheapside.

'Yes, it is the peace here that I love best,' he said as he and Mistress Lopez, a cheerful little woman, much younger than her husband, sat down to supper with their guests in a small dining-parlour. 'You young people were born in England, and you can never know how *I* suffered. The Inquisition drove me from my homeland, and now I shall never see Portugal again.'

'But you are greatly respected in England, sir,' said Robin, looking admiringly at the splendid array of silver and gold on the plate cupboard, the rich tapestries on the walls and the fine damask on the table, and thinking that not even Master Mendes had so grand a house.

'Of course he is respected here,' said Mistress Lopez proudly. 'My husband is the most learned doctor in the whole of Europe. Any country would be glad to offer him hospitality.'

'My dear . . .' said Dr Lopez with a reproving little smile, but his wife ignored the interruption and went on quickly: 'He was house physician at St Bartholomew's Hospital for many years, and he has had many famous people among his patients . . . the late Lord Leicester and Sir Francis Walsingham, God rest them – yes, they are dead now, but he would have saved them if he could – and now, of course . . .' She did not finish the sentence, but the children knew to whom she was referring.

'Oh please, Dr Lopez, do tell us about the Queen,' said Frances eagerly. 'Is she ill a great deal?'

'Hardly ever. I am glad to say.'

'Then *that* means you don't see her very often.'

Dr Lopez's eyes twinkled. 'Her Majesty is graciously pleased to number me among her friends,' he said. 'I sometimes dine at Court, and my wife and I are always invited to the Christmas revels and other entertainments. Why, the Queen even wears a ruby ring that I once gave her, and no token of friendship can be greater than that.'

The children gazed at the old man, their eyes shining.

'Then she must think of you every time she sees it,' cried Frances.

'Her Majesty is more likely to think of me whenever she sees medicine,' replied Dr Lopez.

'Which is her favourite medicine?'

'Why, little maid, she has no favourites – being wise, she hates them all. I have no doubt she hides all my potions and throws them out of the window as soon as I am gone – or feeds them to her maids of honour, perhaps. I hope it is not treason to say so, but I sometimes think the Queen is the worst patient in Christendom.'

30

'My mother once made me eat a chopped mouse when I had the toothache,' Frances went on, 'and it didn't cure my toothache but it *did* make me sick. Do you ever give the Queen chopped mice?'

'No, I value my life too well,' replied Dr Lopez. 'Chopped mouse is a common remedy – any housewife can lay hands on a mouse. Other cures are more rare and expensive. Did you know, for instance, that dragon's fat is said to be a cure for ulcers? Or that the blood of an elephant mingled with the ashes of a weasel can cure leprosy? Or that a unicorn's horn is an excellent antidote to poison?'

'But where do you get your dragons and unicorns?' asked Robin eagerly.

'I don't know,' replied the doctor, laughing. 'I have never prescribed them yet . . . not even to the Queen. I prefer to use simpler remedies. As soon as we have finished our supper you must come and see my herb garden . . . or rather, my wife's herb garden, for she looks after it for me. There is a cure there for every ailment in the world.'

The sun was setting as the doctor led his young guests through the knot garden, which was threaded with neatly-clipped hedges in geometrical designs, towards a shady plot where herbs, dark green and silvery, spiky and feathery, filled the air with a perfume more intense than that of flowers.

'There's rosemary, that is to cure envy, and a bedtime drink made with thyme will soothe ambition,' said the doctor, smiling to himself as he pointed out the various plants. 'Then there's basil, which cures pride, and sweet marjoram, which heals disappointment . . .'

'Sir, you must be jesting,' said Philip indignantly.

Dr Lopez looked down at him, his eyes merry. 'If I were to tell you the true use of these herbs,' he said, 'then you would be as wise as I am, and perhaps you would be the Queen's physician instead of me. But now we must go indoors again – my wife has sweetmeats waiting for us, and we are both longing to hear Robin's music.'

The dining-parlour, lit by a log fire and a dozen tall wax candles in heavy silver candlesticks, seemed warm and a little stuffy after the cool fragrance of the garden. A servant brought in a silver flagon of wine and a tray of gingerbread, marchpane, sugared apricots, candied violets and rose-petals. The marchpane, which was a wonderful confection of ground almonds, sugar and rose-water, looked too beautiful to eat, for Mistress Lopez had covered it with tiny sugar birds and animals and traced a pattern on it in gilding and caraway seeds.

I'm not going to make beautiful things like that for Thomas Mendes to guzzle when I'm a wife, thought Frances sulkily. It's all very well for Mistress Lopez . . . she loves her husband. I wonder if she was forced to marry him. She glanced at Mistress Lopez's rosy, beaming face as it bent over the tray of sweetmeats, and decided that she had married Dr Lopez of her own free will.

But Frances was not allowed to brood for long. Robin was invited to bring out his lute, and while Dr Lopez accompanied him on the Viol de Gambo and Mistress Lopez sat embroidering a cushion with daisies in gold and silver thread, he played and sang the madrigal he had composed in honour of Mother's birthday:

> 'Sweet Madam, wake;
> This is your day of birth,
> And all the green and springing earth
> Is merry for your sake . . .'

Robin faltered a little at this point, for the door of the dining-parlour had opened very slightly and a face seemed to be watching him through the crack. A dark face, with something sombre and suspicious about the eyes. Then the

32

door closed again and the face vanished, leaving Robin to wonder if he had imagined it.

He sang on, his voice trembling a little.

'Bravo!' cried Dr Lopez when the song had ended. 'I think some of our Court composers had better look to their pensions.' He seemed cheerful and at ease; it was obvious that he had not seen any dark face at the door.

After Robin had sung three more of his songs to much applause, Dr Lopez suggested a part-song. He chose 'Falconers Lure', and even Mistress Lopez – protesting that she could not sing a note – was persuaded to join in. All went well until Mistress Lopez's shrill voice cracked on the highest 'Lu-u-ure', and the whole company collapsed into laughter.

It was while they were laughing, and Dr Lopez was patting his wife consolingly on the shoulder, that the door opened and the dark face appeared again. This time it did not vanish, but looked at Dr Lopez enquiringly.

'Signor Ferreira,' said the doctor quickly, 'you see that I am occupied with guests.'

The newcomer shrugged his shoulders and advanced into the room. He was a thin young man, dressed in a slightly threadbare doublet of black velvet. A piece of crumpled parchment was clutched in his hand.

'Signor Ferreira,' repeated Dr Lopez, his voice a little impatient now, 'if you have any business to discuss with me, may we leave it till later?'

The young man held out the piece of parchment towards the doctor.

'Your pardon, sir,' he said, speaking in a heavy Portuguese accent. 'But my business is urgent, so I thought I might take the liberty . . . I have received this letter from Flanders, and it must have an immediate reply . . .'

Dr Lopez's face darkened with anger. 'At least let us go into another room,' he said brusquely. 'How long have you been in the habit of discussing your master's secret affairs in front of strangers?' He took Signor Ferreira by the sleeve and pulled him out of the room, and the door slammed after them.

The children looked enquiringly at Mistress Lopez, who had turned pale.

'He . . . Signor Ferreira lodges with us,' she stammered at last. 'He is one of Dom Antonio's gentlemen.'

'Dom Antonio?' said Robin, thinking that the name sounded familiar. Then suddenly he remembered the Seder table at the Mendes's house, and Dr Lopez telling how he and the Earl of Essex were plotting to restore the Pretender Dom Antonio to the throne of Portugal.

'Poor young man . . . he has been ruined through his devotion to Dom Antonio's cause,' Mistress Lopez went on. 'If it were not for my husband's generosity, he would have starved to death by now. But Dr Lopez is always ready to help compatriots who have fallen on hard times.'

If that were so, thought Robin, Mistress Lopez should be happy. Why, then, did she seem so nervous?

Suddenly, from just outside the room, there came the sound of angry voices raised in what seemed to be a quarrel. Although the door was closed, the children could make out the words quite easily. Dr Lopez was shouting, 'Away, you will get us all hanged unless you learn discretion,' to which Signor Ferreira replied, 'Never fear, sir, you are a loyal servant of Spain, and I am sure King Philip knows that.'

Robin felt his blood run cold. A loyal servant of Spain . . . and Spain was the enemy of England. Could it be possible that Dr Lopez was a traitor? He saw Mistress Lopez clutch at her throat. He saw Philip and Frances gazing at him wide-eyed. All at once it seemed to him that the beautiful room where they had passed so pleasant an evening had become ugly, that the marchpane tasted sickly, and that the sweet music had grown discordant.

After a few moments Dr Lopez came back into the room.

34

Though he tried to seem calm and cheerful, the children could tell that he was angry.

'It was only a trivial thing after all . . .' he began, and then broke off as he caught sight of his wife's distraught face. 'Why, Catherine, my dear, what is it?'

'They heard,' said Mistress Lopez. 'These children heard everything. They heard Signor Ferreira call you a loyal servant of Spain.' Her face crumpled, and she burst into tears. 'Oh, why do you have to meddle in State affairs? Isn't it enough that you are the Queen's physician?'

Dr Lopez looked at the children, and then sat down heavily.

'I see that I shall have to confide in you,' he said after a few minutes, 'or else you will truly believe me to be a traitor.'

And then he explained that he was in fact leading a double life . . . that he was working in the service of England while pretending to be in the pay of Spain.

'It was Sir Francis Walsingham, our late Secretary of State, God rest his soul, who asked me to lend my name to certain proceedings,' Dr Lopez went on. 'He sent a spy to King Philip on the pretext of arranging a peace treaty, and it was agreed that the letters to the King should appear to come from me . . .'

'But why from you, sir?' asked Robin, puzzled.

'Because I have some influence with the Queen. We made it seem that *I* was anxious to see friendship between our two countries . . . that I was persuading Her Majesty towards the idea of peace.'

'And King Philip still believes that?'

'Of course. He also believes that I am working against Dom Antonio, who – as you know – is the enemy of Spain.'

'But I thought you and my Lord Essex were plotting to restore Dom Antonio to his throne,' said Robin.

'Ah, you overheard that at the Seder, I suppose?' replied Dr Lopez with a little laugh. 'The truth is that I am working

35

neither for nor against Dom Antonio. For reasons of expedi-
ency I let Lord Essex believe that I am working *for* Dom
Antonio, and King Philip believe that I am working *against*
him. In that way I maintain friends on both sides.'

'And Signor Ferreira . . .'

'Signor Ferreira was a follower of Dom Antonio, but he
has broken with his master and is now working for Spain.
He believes me to be a servant of Spain, as you just heard.
By pretending to be in league with him I obtain much useful
information about Spanish plots against England . . .'

'Then you are really a hero?' interrupted Frances eagerly.

'Not a hero. Just a true subject of the Queen's Majesty.'

'Does the Queen know about it?' asked Philip.

'The Queen knows nothing. It was a secret between
Walsingham and myself.'

'But surely all this must be very dangerous for you, sir,'
said Robin. Then he saw Mistress Lopez grow paler still, and
felt sorry that he had spoken.

'Why dangerous?' asked Dr Lopez.

'Well . . . I mean . . . suppose our people found out that
you were writing to King Philip? Suppose the Queen found
out? Might they not believe that you were *really* in the pay
of Spain?'

Dr Lopez laughed and patted Robin's shoulder.

'My dear lad, there *is* no danger,' he said. 'Would our
Queen really believe me to be a traitor? Haven't I been her
loyal servant for nearly forty years?'

'That's four times as long as I've been alive,' said Philip,
nodding wisely.

'Besides,' the doctor went on, with a reassuring glance at
his wife, 'why should I want to betray the country that gave
me shelter and so much prosperity? What could I hope to
gain from being a traitor? Look around you. I have everything any man could wish for. I have a fine house, a great
fortune and a noble profession; I have an honoured position

36

at Court; my son is being educated at Winchester and will also have a high position in society . . . and I have all these things by courtesy of the Queen. Why should I risk throwing it all away? For what? For a smile and a nod from King Philip? For a pension from him, perhaps? Who in his right mind could possibly believe me to be a traitor?'

'But suppose someone wanted to harm you?' asked Robin.

'My dear boy, no one wants to harm me. I am an old man and I make my living by healing the sick. How could I have enemies? No . . . no, let's have a cup of wine and another song and forget all about these dull affairs of State. By the way, I must ask you to say nothing about what you have learned tonight – not even to your parents.'

'Of course not, sir,' said the children, delighted at the thought of sharing a secret with the Queen's physician.

'Good, good. And now, Robin, I should like to hear your mother's birthday madrigal again. I thought it quite beautiful.'

The rest of the evening passed very pleasantly. At nine o'clock Dr Lopez called one of his servants to escort the children home, for London could be a dangerous place at night. The narrow streets were haunted by robbers and cut-throats, and there was always the risk of slipping in the mire or falling into a rubbish heap in the dark. Besides, the city gates were locked at nightfall, and the watchman would open up only for someone of consequence . . . such as a servant of the Queen's physician.

The streets were very dark as the children walked back towards St Olave's, accompanied by a burly serving-man carrying a flaring torch. Sometimes they passed an open window ablaze with candles; sometimes a little group of singing gallants ambled past on their way home from a supper or a tavern, followed by a link-boy with a torch or lantern. But apart from these infrequent bursts of light the streets were black and damp, only an occasional glimmer showing through a chink in a door or window-shutter, and the badly-paved lanes squelching and stinking underfoot. There seemed to be terrifying shadows lurking under the overhanging fronts of the houses, and once Robin thought he heard a scuffle and a groan coming from some darkened alley as they passed.

The children were glad to reach St Olave's at last. They answered all their parents' questions about their visit to Dr Lopez, leaving out, of course, the most important thing of all, and then went happily to bed.

'Wasn't it exciting?' said Philip, as he and Robin snuggled into their feather pillows. 'I think Dr Lopez is a wonderful man. D'you think he might take us to meet the Queen one day?'

Robin grunted drowsily, picturing the fine house in Holborn and the doctor's clever, kindly face. But for some reason he kept thinking of Signor Ferreira, and when at last he fell asleep he dreamed he saw those dark eyes watching him.

Chapter Four

A week later, rehearsals started for *Romeo and Juliet*, and Robin stopped brooding over Dr Lopez and his sinister lodger.

His worries were still not over, however, for Father was not altogether pleased at the idea of all the schooling he was going to miss on account of the play. 'First there are the rehearsals, and then the production itself may be a success and run for several weeks, Heaven forbid!' he grumbled. 'I do not pay school fees so that you may grow up an untutored ruffian. If it were not that Dr Lopez had persuaded me to let you appear in the play . . .'

Robin silently blessed Dr Lopez, and assured Father that most of the rehearsals would take place during the Easter holidays: that he would not have to miss morning school during the run of the play, since theatre performances took place in the afternoon, and that he would study hard at home in the evenings to make up for any lessons he might lose.

The morning of the first rehearsal dawned bright and sunny. Robin was too excited to eat any breakfast; he had the feeling that he was on the brink of an exciting new life, and he felt sorry for Philip, who had to go to school as usual.

He was to meet Richard Lucy at Blackfriars, and they were to take a boat to Bankside, in Southwark, where the theatre stood. Robin had never travelled in a boat before, and when he arrived at the edge of the Thames he again found himself gazing wide-eyed at its beauty and splendour. Its waters were as bright as silver, so clear that he could see the fish leaping and twisting in its lower depths, and edged along the North shore with gardens and orchards, stately mansions and a hundred thickly-clustering church spires. River craft rode past in a long and crowded procession, galleons with painted sails bearing precious cargoes to and from distant lands, private pleasure-boats with brightly-striped canopies, and busy little brown barges like the one in which he and Richard were to travel. It seemed to Robin that there were more people on the river than in the streets. But the Thames was not entirely inhabited by boats and passengers, for every so often a flock of swans would glide past, resting like snowy clouds on the crystal water.

'You don't have a river like this in Bristol, do you?' said Richard wickedly as the boys handed their penny fare to the boatman and stepped into the barge. Robin did not even bother to reply; he was too busy gazing at all the further wonders that were revealed as the boat drew away from the shore and advanced into the middle of the river. To his left he could see the full span of London Bridge, lined along its entire length with splendid houses and shops, chapels and arches and turrets. Behind him, to the right, lay the Strand with its noble palaces, the homes of Dukes and Earls, and the Temple Gardens ablaze with flowers, and the distant pinnacles of the Queen's Palace of Whitehall. Before him, on the South Bank, lay the world he had never yet seen, the world of theatres and bear-gardens and cockpits, taverns and prisons, pleasure and sin.

'My father says Southwark is an evil place to visit,' said Robin contentedly as the opposite shore of the river came into view.

'Evil? Why, all the best entertainment in London is to be found here,' replied Richard. 'Have you ever seen a bear-baiting?'

'No.'

'Then you don't know what you've missed. Bear-baitings are great fun, and so are cock-fights. Even the Queen goes to them. We'll see one after the rehearsal, if we have time. They have them at Paris Garden, which is quite near the Rose Theatre.'

A few moments later the boat arrived at the Paris Garden landing-stairs, and Robin looked about with interest at the marshy shore and the clustered buildings which were considered so wicked by his father and so exciting by Richard Lucy and the Queen. The walls were plastered with playbills advertising all kinds of entertainments, and Robin's heart leaped at the sight of a poster which announced, in large scarlet letters, that the Lord Chamberlain's Men would be presenting *Romeo and Juliet*, a marvellous new tragedy by Will Shakespeare, at the Rose Theatre on the fourth of May.

A short walk brought the boys to the Rose, and Robin, who had never seen a theatre before, looked about him eagerly. It was a circular building, open to the sky and surrounded by three roofed galleries, and looking very like the yards of the inns where the Fernandez family had stayed overnight during their journey from Bristol to London. On the roof was a turret from which a flame-coloured silk flag hung limply.

'They will run it up before the performance begins,' Richard explained, 'and people will see it from far and wide and know that there is a play at the theatre. And then they will come flocking to see us . . .'

Just then a boy came up behind Richard and tapped him on the shoulder. 'Are you the lads from the choir-school?' he asked.

Richard replied that they were.

'Master Shakespeare asked me to meet you and bring you to the tiring-house,' said the boy. 'They're all in there. We're to start rehearsing in half an hour, after Master Burbage has finished his breakfast and they've done arguing.'

'What are they arguing about?' asked Robin, alarmed.

'The cost of Master Burbage's new cloak,' said the boy, laughing.

'Are *you* one of the actors?' said Robin eagerly.

'I am. My name is Nicholas Tooley,' replied the boy, stopping to make a graceful little bow. He was about twelve, slim and slight, with fair hair and delicate features.

'And what part do you play?' asked Richard.

'Oh, I'm to be Juliet,' replied Nicholas. 'I'm playing all the heroines this season. Just wait till Master Burbage hears how much my bridal gown is going to cost – satin has doubled in price since last year!'

'Who is this Master Burbage?' asked Robin curiously.

'He's the chief actor and manager of the company, of course,' said Richard before Nicholas could answer. '*And* he owns the Theatre in Shoreditch, the first real theatre ever built in England. I thought everyone knew that.'

'Does the Rose also belong to him?' asked Robin, ignoring the gibe.

'No, this theatre belongs to Master Henshawe and Master Alleyn,' Nicholas replied. 'The Theatre is closed just now because of the pestilence, so Master Alleyn has let us borrow the Rose for our new production. He and Master Burbage are friends, in spite of their being rivals. But that is the way it always is in the theatre.'

While the boys were talking, Nicholas led the newcomers across the yard of the theatre, where the groundlings paid a penny to stand and watch the play, and up on to a huge raised square stage with red curtains drawn across the back and a massive pillar on either side. The pillars supported a roof-like structure, its underside painted blue and adorned with a gilded sun and moon and studded with silver stars, and Nicholas pointed out that this was the 'Heavens', which stood in for a night sky when one was needed, since the performances all took place by day.

There was a door to one side of the stage, and through it the boys could hear a babble of voices and laughter. It led directly into the tiring-house, where the company sat eating and arguing, drinking and snatching last-minute glances at their scripts. Will Shakespeare looked up as the door opened, and greeted the boys with a cheerful wave.

'It's Master Lucy and my Rosaline,' he cried. 'Come in and meet your new colleagues. I dare say you're happy to be off school today, but you'll find that Master Burbage treats you worse than your schoolmaster ever dared.'

Master Burbage's mouth was full of pie, so he merely nodded loftily at the boys, who made him a polite little bow. He was a tall, imposing-looking man with a neat, dark beard and flashing eyes.

'Do you know your lines?' he asked, as soon as he could speak.

'They have no lines,' replied Will Shakespeare, seeing the boys glancing at him nervously. 'Master Lucy is to sing a solo at the masked ball, and Master Fernandez plays Rosaline in mime. I'm sorry Robin . . . I know I promised to write you some lines, but the play has already been approved by the Master of the Revels, and the script mustn't be altered or added to in any way once he has given it a licence.'

Just then the door opened, and a magnificent figure strode in. He wore a doublet of crimson velvet and embroidered with gold, breeches of yellow satin, an enormous three-piled ruff edged with pearls, a blue velvet cloak faced with flame-coloured taffeta, and a beaver hat as tall as a steeple and adorned with ostrich feathers. Master Burbage's face darkened with rage at the sight of this splendid apparition. He put down his tankard and bellowed: 'William Slye, how often have I told you *not* to wear your stage clothes outside the theatre?'

'I . . . I'm sorry, Dick,' stammered Master Slye, 'but I went to supper last night with some fine company – Lord Fairmont and his friends – and I . . .'

'You wanted to show off in front of them, like the fool that you are! Well, I'll not have you wearing stage costumes to impress your friends, even if they be Dukes and Earls. In the first place, these clothes have been made at great expense and I won't have them ruined at gluttonous suppers and drunken carousings, and in the second place, the public won't pay to see them in the theatre if they can see them for nothing in the tavern. So you're fined a shilling, and if it happens again it will be half a crown. Now go away, popinjay, and put on your old breeches.'

Robin had been listening to all this with great enjoyment, thinking that it was a great deal more fun than sitting in a schoolroom. As soon as Master Slye had slunk gloomily away to change his clothes, he turned to Will Shakespeare and asked eagerly, 'When do we start rehearsing, sir?'

'In a little while,' replied Master Shakespeare. 'In the meantime, how would you like to come upstairs to wardrobe and storage and see something of our costumes and properties?'

'Oh yes please, sir,' said Robin and Richard, their eyes shining with such excitement that Nicholas, who had seen it all before, asked if he might come too.

A sound of hammering and a pungent smell of paint and glue and varnish greeted them as Master Shakespeare opened

44

the door of wardrobe and storage. Robin stepped through, and found himself in a magic land.

One corner of the room was hideous with coffins and a great heap of skulls and bones; in another corner glinted a gold throne, royal crowns, splendid jewels and a mass of gleaming armour, swords and spears and halberds; in a third corner a cauldron large enough to boil a man alive, several mossy banks, a bay tree and a snake, and a severed head which lay glaring at the ceiling with its painted eyes. In the middle of the room two workmen were constructing what looked like a tomb; this was the hammering sound the boys had heard. Beyond the storage room lay the wardrobe, crammed with costumes of unbelievable splendour, made of cloth of gold, satin and velvet, damask and taffeta in brilliant shades of blue and green, crimson, scarlet and purple, stitched with gems and trimmed with gold and silver lace or tinsel.

'That's mine,' squealed Nicholas, pointing at a beautiful white satin gown which was having its hem lavishly embroidered with artificial pearls. 'That's the bridal gown I'm to have as Juliet.'

'And a pretty penny it cost us,' growled the tailor who was working on it. 'But we'll get our money's worth out of it, never fear. After it has been worn by half a dozen pretty heroines it will be cut down to make the lining for a cloak. Then it will become a goddess's tunic, and then perhaps a ship's sail, and finally a peasant woman's kerchief or a Cupid's loincloth . . . Oh, nothing gets wasted here, believe me.'

'But why are the costumes so expensive?' asked Robin. 'They are much grander than anything I ever saw in real life.'

'Why lad, they have to be, to give the playgoer his money's worth,' replied Will Shakespeare with a laugh. 'We can't give the poor fellow real castles or palaces or galleons or battle-fields, or thunder or lightning; all we can give him are fine words and finer costumes, and the costumes cost a great deal more than the words. Now I, as the author, am paid five pounds for a play, or six if I'm lucky, but some of these cloaks cost twenty pounds apiece. And quite right too . . . No one is going to come and spend a hard-earned fourpence just to gape at Master Burbage's old breeches.'

Robin was just about to say that he thought Master Shakespeare was shamefully underpaid when the property-master appeared and asked if the boys would like to see the hut above the 'Heavens'. This was the place where the machinery for special effects was kept, and Robin watched open-mouthed as the old man showed them the pulley by which gods and goddesses, nymphs and sprites were lowered from the sky.

'This is the most marvellous magic of all,' thought Robin, closing his eyes and seeing radiant beings, clothed in rosy light, descending out of imaginary clouds towards the dazzled eyes of the groundlings.

But when the rehearsal began, Robin knew better. He learned then that the most marvellous magic of all was not in the costumes, or in the pulley-borne gods and goddesses, but in the words.

In all his life he had never heard such language, and he listened, entranced, as the actors read aloud from their scripts:

> 'Her chariot is an empty hazel-nut,
> Made by the joiner squirrel or old grub,
> Time out of mind the fairies' coachmakers.
> And in this state she gallops night by night
> Through lovers' brains, and then they
>   dream of love . . .'

'That's much too long, Will,' broke in Master Burbage, interrupting Mercutio's soliloquy and Robin's reverie both at the same time. 'That's your trouble . . . you always over-write . . .'

Secretly Robin thought that the play, with its exciting scenes of family vendetta and its beautiful scenes of tragic love, was not half long enough! He also found himself longing for some of those wonderful words to say. All at once the part of Rosaline, with its mimed flirting and head-tossing, seemed very unsatisfying, and he envied Nicholas Tooley. It was strange, Nicholas had up till that time been no more than an ordinary, untidy schoolboy with wrinkled hose and a catapult in his pouch, but when he spoke Juliet's lines his face seemed to change, and his voice became gentle and beautiful, like a young girl's.

Perhaps, thought Robin hopefully, Nicholas might have an accident, just a slight accident, and I might, by some miracle, be called on to play the part. I shall never rest till I can be apprenticed to this company. Any fool can be a merchant, but to be an actor . . . that would be everything I have ever dreamed of. Father must understand that . . . he *must*.

When the dinner-break came, Robin approached Will Shakespeare shyly, almost afraid to speak to someone he now knew to be so talented.

'It's a lovely play, sir,' he said. 'You're a very good writer.'

Will Shakespeare swallowed a mouthful of egg and bacon pie, and looked back at Robin gravely.

'It's kind of you to say so,' he replied. 'Would you like a piece of pie?'

Robin shook his head and left quickly, before Master Shakespeare could begin to wonder why he had refused.

When the day's rehearsal was over, Richard Lucy turned eagerly to Robin and Nicholas.

'Shall we be off to see the bear-baiting?' he asked. 'It's

early yet, and it would be a pity to be on Bankside and miss it.'

'Why not?' replied Robin. 'Today is my day for new experiences.'

The bear-baiting arena at Paris Garden was, like the theatre, round and open to the sky, but there the resemblance ended. Here was no silken flag, no gilded 'Heavens' or pulley-borne gods and goddesses, no bejewelled costumes and no splendid words . . . only a great deal of sawdust and blood, the monstrous great bear struggling to evade the snapping jaws of the mastiffs, and the roaring delight of the crowd. There were a number of gallants and even some pretty ladies in the audience, and they seemed to be enjoying themselves hugely.

But Robin soon discovered that *he* was not enjoying it at all. It seemed a cruel sport; all the blood and growling made him feel sick, and once, when the bear seized an unfortunate dog in his great fangs and crushed his head as though it were an apple, he nearly got up and ran out of the arena.

But of course he could not, for Richard was cheering lustily and Nicholas's eyes were alight with glee, and how could he seem different? Robin looked at Nicholas, and wondered how he could so lately have been Juliet, whispering sweet words to her lover.

'Get him!' yelled Nicholas. 'Tear his throat out!' and his cry was taken up by a thousand other voices.

When the show was over and the boys finally emerged from the bear-pit, Nicholas looked at Robin and laughed.

'You're as pale as a cream cheese,' he said. 'Aren't you feeling well?'

'Robin's never seen a bear-baiting before,' Richard explained. 'Did you enjoy it, Robin?'

'Not very much,' Robin mumbled.

'Why not? It's marvellous sport.'

'It's cruel.'

48

'No, it's not. Bears and dogs aren't people . . . they can't feel anything.'

'I like the theatre better,' said Robin firmly.

'But bear-baiting is real and the theatre is only pretence,' Nicholas chimed in. 'How can anything which is only pretence be better?'

Robin was so shocked to hear those words from a professional actor that, if he had not at that moment seen Will Shakespeare coming out of the Bell and Cock, he would probably have stayed silent all the way back to St Olave's. But Master Shakespeare was here, the script of *Romeo and Juliet* still poking out of his pouch, and Robin was so happy to see him that he almost cried out.

'We've been to the bear-baiting,' cried Richard before Master Shakespeare could even speak. 'It was Robin's first time, and he was nearly sick.'

'I'm not surprised,' replied Master Shakespeare. 'I sometimes feel sick myself.'

'Don't you enjoy bear-baitings, Will?' asked Nicholas in astonishment. 'I've seen you at the bear-pit many times.'

'Oh yes, but I go to study the audience, not the animals.'

'It's cruel,' repeated Robin, suspecting that he had an ally in Will Shakespeare.

'But the bear can't feel anything,' persisted Richard.

Master Shakespeare laughed and pretended to punch his head.

'That's the trouble with you and nine-tenths of mankind,' he said. 'Why, you cruel little wretch, don't you know that a poor beetle suffers as much when you tread on him as a giant suffers when he dies?'

When Robin arrived back on his own side of the Thames, he remembered that Dr Lopez had invited him to call on him any evening he liked for a game of chess. It was early and his parents were not expecting him home yet; besides, he felt a need for the doctor's understanding company after all the excitements and new experiences of the day. So, after he had said good-bye to Richard, he set off towards Holborn.

As soon as he saw Dr Lopez, Robin had the strange notion that the old man had grown much older during the past week. It was difficult to explain, but it seemed that his face had become more hollow and his shoulders more stooping. And Mistress Lopez also looked different. Her eyes had lost their sparkle and her cheeks their dimples, and she looked as if she were waiting for something frightening to happen. But she and her husband both smiled happily when they saw their visitor. Mistress Lopez called for wine and marchpane then she and Dr Lopez sat down and listened as Robin told them about the theatre, the rehearsal, the marvellous play, and his visit to the bear-pit.

'It was dreadful . . . all that blood, and one of the dogs had his head chewed off,' he said. 'But the worst thing of all was the way the audience enjoyed it. Even the ladies were jumping about and shouting in their beautiful farthingales. Who are they, all these people who come to see animals torn to pieces?'

'Why, these same people who will come to see you perform in *Romeo and Juliet*, and listen in rapture to Master Shakespeare's golden words, and weep to see the lovers die,' said Dr Lopez with a sad little smile. 'These same people who sing madrigals about larks and daisies and unrequited love find music just as sweet in the cries of the tortured. These gallants who deck themselves in embroidered velvets enjoy nothing so much as a really spectacular execution. These gentle souls who write exquisite poetry would come to see you or me hanged at Tyburn without losing any of their appetite for dinner. They will go to see your friend Shakespeare's plays, and then say, "Yes, the language was magnificent, but how much more exciting it would have been if only the blood had been real!" They are scholars and artists, and yet they are savages. This is the great riddle of our age, and *I* am not the one to answer it. But tell me, Robin, when does your play open? I hope I may be able to see it.'

'On the fourth of May,' said Robin, feeling a thrill of excitement creeping once more up his spine. 'Master Shakespeare hopes it may run for six weeks or more, if the public likes it. But after that I shall have to go back to school again, and I can't bear the thought. Real life is never as exciting as the theatre . . .'

Robin broke off as somebody knocked at the front door. It was not a particularly loud or demanding knock, and yet Dr Lopez seemed to shrink at the sound of it.

'Were we expecting any visitors?' he asked his wife, who also appeared to have grown paler.

'It may be my father, or perhaps Dr Nunez . . .' she began, her voice trembling a little.

At that moment a servant came into the room.

'Sir, there are three gentlemen here who say they have been sent by the Earl of Essex,' he announced. 'They are asking for Signor Ferreira.'

Robin had forgotten all about Dr Lopez's dark, sinister guest, but now he remembered, and shuddered.

'Signor Ferreira is in the library,' replied Dr Lopez, obviously trying to speak calmly. 'Please bring the gentlemen here to me, and then go and inform our good friend that he is wanted.'

The servant bowed and left the room, and in a few moments came back with three tall, powerfully-built men, all dressed in sombre black.

'You are welcome, if you come from my friend Essex,' said Dr Lopez with a forced smile. 'Signor Ferreira is in the library. He told me he had a letter to write. I have sent for him.'

51

'Thank you, Dr Lopez,' replied one of the men gravely. 'And to whom is he writing this letter?'

'Sir, you would hardly expect me to interfere with my guests' private correspondence . . .'

'I would, if it were treasonable.'

'Sir, I know of no treason that is being committed under my roof . . .' began the doctor indignantly. Then he broke off, as Signor Ferreira walked into the room.

The tall man moved slowly towards him.

'Are you Esteban Ferreira?' he asked in a solemn voice.

'I am,' replied Signor Ferreira, looking nervous.

The tall man drew a parchment scroll out of his doublet and unrolled it.

'Esteban Ferreira, I have here a warrant for your arrest in the name of Her Most Gracious Majesty Queen Elizabeth,' he said. 'I have been commanded by my Lord Essex to take you to Eton and place you in the custody of Don Antonio, your former master.'

'But this is outrageous,' cried Dr Lopez. 'This man has done no harm. What are the charges against him?'

'My Lord Essex did not favour us with any details,' replied the man with a grim smile. 'All we know is that Signor Ferreira is to be detained for questioning. Who knows, he might be released tomorrow. Or else . . .'

'Or else?'

'He could even be charged with High Treason, Dr Lopez. Lord Essex suspects that he may be in the pay of Spain. But Time alone will tell.'

Chapter Five

Robin felt he ought to be worrying about Dr Lopez and Signor Ferreira, but the next few weeks were so taken up with rehearsals that he had no time to think of anything but the play.

May the fourth arrived at last – a warm day with all the steeples of London glittering in the sunlight. The performance was due to begin at three o'clock, but the cast arrived at the Rose soon after noon. Too excited to eat much dinner, Robin, Richard and Nicholas climbed up to the hut to watch the signal flag being run up the turret. The flame-coloured silk fluttered bravely against the clear blue sky, and the boys cheered.

'You should be taking a last look at your lines instead of fooling about up here,' grumbled the old property-man whose task it was to raise and lower the flag.

'I know all my lines,' said Robin.

Richard giggled, and Nicholas tried to hide his growing nervousness by doing a handstand.

From the hut the boys could see the river and the crowded towers and church spires on the opposite shore. Even as they watched they saw a constant procession of boats, looking as small as ants, leaving the North shore and setting out in the direction of the Paris Garden landing-stairs.

'Here comes our audience,' said Nicholas, swallowing.

'Do you mean they're coming to see *us*?' gasped Robin.

'Who else? We're the only theatre putting on a play this afternoon. Let's hope they're all sober and no one picks a fight in the middle of the balcony scene.'

At this moment one of the actors came up to announce that it was time for them to change into their costumes. The boys followed him to the tiring-house, where great turmoil greeted them. All the actors were there – Master Burbage, who of course played Romeo (though Robin secretly felt he looked too old for the part) whirling his gold satin cloak about him like the wings of a giant moth, and all the boys who played girls' roles grumbling and wriggling as they were fastened into their great hooped petticoats and farthingales with the help of numerous wire pins of all different sizes.

'I had no idea it took a woman so long to dress,' said Robin, as someone fixed a three-piled ruff round his neck and propped it up with a framework of pasteboard and wire. The ruff, combined with his nervousness, made him feel quite sick. He turned to make a face at Nicholas, and then stood still and gasped. Dressed in pale pink satin, with a wig of long golden hair, Nicholas had become a beautiful young girl. Even his face looked different. Robin wondered how he could ever have shouted, 'Get him! Tear his throat out!' in the bloody hubbub of the bear-pit.

In the gallery above the stage the musicians and choristers were beginning to assemble. Through the half-open door of the tiring-house Robin could hear them tuning up their instruments, the occasional shrill murmur of a cornet or reedy twitter of a hautboy sounding like some distant bird in the afternoon sky.

Although it was only half-past two, the audience was already starting to arrive. Peering through the curtains from the place behind the stage, Robin was surprised to see a certain amount of fighting and scuffling going on in the pit, where the groundlings paid a penny each to stand and watch the play. Fruit-sellers wandered round the theatre with baskets of nuts and oranges, and there was a great deal of eating, with much flicking of pips and nutshells towards the roofed galleries where the wealthier patrons sat. Jeers and catcalls greeted the arrival of the occasional dandy in a tall, plumed hat. At one point a party of gallants came in and were shown up on to the stage itself, where they sat playing cards and trying to ignore the rude witticisms that floated up towards them from the pit.

'Where's Will Shakespeare? Is he hiding?' asked Robin, suddenly picturing the playwright – overcome with nerves – concealing himself under a pile of costumes in the tiring-house.

'Hiding? Not he . . . Will loves first performances,' replied Nicholas. 'He's out there with the box.'

'The box?'

'He's down in the audience, taking the entrance-money,' explained Nicholas. 'Look.' And sure enough, following the pointing finger, Robin saw Will Shakespeare, dressed for his role as Benvolio, cheerfully passing among the groundlings with a box of jingling coins.

'This is going to be a miserable play,' grumbled John Rice, who had just joined them. 'There aren't any special effects at all. In our last play we had an angel let down from the Heavens on a throne, a woman struck by lightning, three devils appearing out of a black cloud, and a dragon who came up through the trap-door and ate Master Alleyn.'

Robin did not reply, for he had just seen his parents and Frances taking their seats in one of the covered galleries. His father, for all his avowed dislike of the theatre, had decided that Robin must have the support of his family at this, his first appearance on a stage. Philip was not with them; boys could not get time off from school unless they were themselves performing. Poor Philip, thought Robin, to be tied to a desk and Latin grammar on such an afternoon as this!

There was an unexpected tightness in his throat, and his eyes pricked with tears.

Just then the trumpets sounded; a gradual hush descended on the audience; Will Ostler walked out upon the stage to speak the Prologue, and the play began.

Romeo and Juliet was a success – the company knew that almost from the beginning. Even the noisiest of the groundlings kept absolutely quiet, and when Juliet stabbed herself and fell dead across Romeo's poisoned corpse, such a sobbing and lamenting arose from the audience that the players were nearly deafened. Peering through the curtains, Robin was astonished to see several big fellows with tears pouring down their cheeks, and one (who had been laying about another with his fists before the play began) was actually rolling on the ground in a paroxysm of grief.

But they all recovered their high spirits when the play ended and the dancing began. As all the characters, both living and dead, came back on stage to join in a galliard and a lively capriole, while the musicians and choristers above their heads piped away with the joy of being alive, the audience began to clap and stamp and even sing in time to the music.

Robin's cheeks were still flushed with excitement when he came off-stage and crossed to the gallery to greet his family.

'I suppose this play will run for weeks, and you'll be missing God knows how much precious schooling,' were Father's first words. 'I don't know why I waste so much money on your education.'

'Robin, you look beautiful,' said Mother, ignoring Father's gruffness and giving Robin a great hug. 'I had no idea a farthingale would suit you so well. I know some girls who would give their eyes to look so lovely . . . Mistress Mendoza's daughter for one.'

'Don't talk such nonsense, Gracia,' snapped Father, 'or you'll be encouraging the boy to go about dressed as a girl, and then God knows what will become of him! Now, go and change out of that ridiculous costume at once, and then meet us by the main entrance.'

'Yes, Father,' said Robin obediently. 'Would you like to meet Master Shakespeare and Master Burbage?'

'No, I would not. I've told you before that I will have nothing to do with these tinselled vagabonds of play-actors. Now, hurry!'

The tiring-house was full of noise and jollity and joyful congratulations, and Robin wished he could stay and join in the fun. But his family were waiting for him, so he hurried out of his farthingale and back to his own clothes and said a last good-bye to his friends.

'I thought it was a lovely play,' said Frances shyly, as the family stepped aboard its boat at the Paris Garden landing-stage. Father had hired one of the more expensive tilt-boats, and the children gazed up in admiration at the red-and-white striped canopy as it swayed and billowed above them.

'Will Shakespeare is a very clever man,' replied Robin, a little wistful now as Bankside began to glide away from him across the shining water.

'I cried all through the last scene, especially when Juliet stabbed herself,' added Frances. 'Was the blood real?'

'Of course. It was sheep's blood. They always use real

57

blood in plays. Nicholas Tooley tells me that when they did *The Battle of Alcazar* one of the characters had to be disembowelled, and they used a sheep's liver, heart and lungs. He said it looked so realistic that the audience screamed . . .' Here Robin broke off, seeing that Father was looking at him disapprovingly.

'Did you feel nervous while you were acting?' asked Mother quickly.

'Not at all. I could hardly believe it. As soon as I stepped on to the stage I felt as though I belonged there . . .' Robin looked at Father's lowering brow and realized that he had once more said the wrong thing.

There was a long pause, and then Father said, 'Let this be understood, my boy. I allowed you to take part in this play because Dr Lopez persuaded me, but I have no intention of letting you make the stage your livelihood. As soon as you reach your fourteenth birthday you are to be apprenticed to the Grocers' Guild, and then there will be no time for all this theatrical nonsense.'

So I have just sixteen months left, thought Robin, as he huddled back among the striped cushions of the boat. Sixteen more glorious months before I give up the rest of my life to soap and spices. But anything could happen in that time. Dr Lopez might even persuade my father to change his mind . . .

Across the widening river he could still see the turret of the Rose Theatre faintly etched on the horizon. Even as he watched he saw the flame-coloured flag run down the pole and sink to rest among the crowded rooftops.

Dr Lopez came to see the play a week later. Robin was overjoyed, but when they met after the performance he was shocked to see how pale and careworn the old man was looking.

'You were very good,' said the doctor kindly. 'As Master

Shakespeare has already observed, you have a natural talent. I hope he will give you a speaking part in his next play.'

'I don't think my father would allow me to take it,' said Robin with a sad little smile. 'He says I may appear as a chorister if I like, but he despises actors.'

'Life is too short for that kind of stupid prejudice,' said the doctor with a sigh. 'But don't tell your father I said so. I would have come to see your play earlier, but I have had many cares and worries lately.'

'Sir, what has happened to Signor Ferreira?' asked Robin, suddenly overcome with guilt at not having enquired sooner. 'Has he been released?'

'Released? No, not he. Hardly any man, once taken, is ever released. He is being held at Eton, where they question him daily, though no actual charges have been brought against him. I went to the Queen to plead for him, but she treated me so coldly. *Very* coldly, for her . . . up till now she has always heard me out with great courtesy.'

'Perhaps she was angry about something else,' said Robin hopefully. 'Perhaps she had the stomach-ache.'

'If she had the stomach-ache she would have asked me for medicine,' said Dr Lopez with a faint twinkle, 'instead of sending me away with a Royal flea in my ear. No, I must confess I am worried. It is not only the Queen who is cold. The Earl of Essex, my good friend, also seems to have turned against me. I met him as I was leaving the Queen's chamber . . . I have met him twice more since then, and he did not even greet me. It was as if I did not exist.'

'Wasn't it Lord Essex who arrested Signor Ferreira?' asked Robin.

'It was, it was. You have a good memory, my boy. He may well have discovered that I am not on Don Antonio's side after all. Lord Essex is a good friend to Don Antonio.'

'He wouldn't try to harm you, would he, sir?' asked Robin anxiously.

'Of course not. I am an old man and an old friend. I was his stepfather's physician – Lord Leicester's physician. Why should he wish to harm me? Besides, he is a good-hearted young man . . . he has a heart of gold. I know it. But enough of my troubles – let's talk of more pleasant things. When are you coming to play chess with me again? My son has gone to spend his school holidays with friends in Norfolk, and my wife and I are longing for young company about the house.'

Robin promised to come soon, and Dr Lopez looked happier as he left. But watching the frail old figure limping away, Robin was seized with a fear he could not explain.

Romeo and Juliet played for six weeks, and though Father complained at the amount of school work he was missing, Robin felt he had never been happier. He loved the carefree life and comradeship of the theatre; he loved the acting, the music and dancing and applause, and the play excited him each time he saw it.

One day, Will Shakespeare took him to one side after the performance.

'The first time I saw you I knew you were a born actor,' he said, 'and your playing here as Rosaline has convinced me. Even Dick Burbage thinks so, and no one is harder to please than our Dick. Now, have you asked your father if he would be willing to let you make the theatre your career?'

Sadly, Robin explained that he was to be apprenticed to the Grocers' Guild and then join the Mendes business, and that his father hated the theatre anyway and would never allow his son to go on the stage.

'It's a pity to see talent go to waste,' said Master Shakespeare, 'and I can't imagine you selling pepper and perfume. My own father was a prosperous merchant – a glover – and a dealer in fine leather, and he was a town councillor and a magistrate besides; and one of the most respected men in Stratford-on-Avon. Of course he wanted me to follow his trade. But I had seen the strolling players as a child each time they came to Stratford . . . and I knew there was only one way of life for me. So I dared my father's anger, and I left my wife and children, and I came to London to be an actor.'

'Your wife and children?' said Robin, surprised. 'I didn't know you were married.'

'Oh yes, I have a wife and family back in Stratford . . . that's a small town in Warwickshire, where I was born. I've three children – two girls, Susanna and Judith, and a boy called Hamnet. Judith and Hamnet are twins, nearly nine years old. Leaving them is the only regret I have. I've seen them only once in the past five years.'

'But, sir, why did you have to leave them?' asked Robin, horrified. 'Why didn't they come with you to London?'

'My wife is a Puritan,' replied Master Shakespeare with a wry smile. 'She thinks the theatre is a snare of Satan and a pit of wickedness, and she looks on me as a lost soul. *Your* father is not a Puritan, by any chance?'

'N-no, sir,' said Robin hastily, unwilling to let the conversation stray to the subject of religion. 'It's just that he thinks it's not seemly for a . . . for his son to be an actor. He thinks all actors are ne'er-do-wells . . . he calls them tinselled vagabonds – ' Here Robin broke off quickly, afraid Will Shakespeare might be offended, but he only laughed.

'Well, perhaps he may still be talked round. Our apprentices are well cared for. They are housed and fed by the best men in our company and made to learn their lessons and say their prayers. I can't take an apprentice myself, having no household of my own, but Dick Burbage has young Nicholas Tooley apprenticed to him and could surely find room for you, and John Heminges keeps many apprentices in addition to his own fourteen children. Luckily he has a large house. Whenever I go there I feel as if I were in a bear-garden.'

Robin thought enviously about John Heminges' house, full of children and song and theatrical japes and jollity. Then

61

he thought of his own house, sedate and orderly and always filled with secret rites and the fear of discovery, and he sighed.

But as he was walking home from the theatre that afternoon, something occurred to him.

I can't become an apprentice, he thought, not if it means living away from home. It would mean having to say Christian prayers and eat forbidden food. It would mean not keeping the Sabbath or the Festivals. It would mean having to keep a watch on my tongue day and night. Just suppose . . . suppose I were to talk in my sleep! I might say something wrong, and betray our whole community. No, no, I can't be apprenticed to the players. It would mean I couldn't go on being a Jew.

He was almost home when another thought came to him:

But what does it mean, after all, to be Jewish? It's nothing but secret worship, and fear, and suffering. We get no joy out of it. Why *should* I have to sacrifice my whole life to a religion that is forbidden by the law of the land?

Robin at once felt guilty for these wicked thoughts and hurriedly asked God to forgive him. But he still could not help thinking of John Heminges' household, where fourteen children and a succession of merry apprentices learned to fence and dance and recite Will Shakespeare's poetry in a house as noisy as a bear-garden.

The Fernandez family were sitting at table one Friday evening, and Father was about to recite the Sabbath benediction over the wine and bread, when there came a knock at the front door.

The Sabbath had come in at sundown, and would end next day when the first three stars appeared in the sky. Mother had lit the ceremonial candles in their heavy silver candlesticks and recited the appropriate blessings. Father had asked God to make his children like their great Biblical ancestors, and had compared his wife to King Solomon's woman of worth, whose price was far above rubies. He had said, 'The Lord make His face to shine upon thee, and be gracious unto thee; the Lord turn His face unto thee and give thee peace.' And now the peace was shattered; the Sabbath ended, perhaps, before it had even begun.

Father and Mother stared at each other, and then at the children, all the blood draining from their faces. They had not been expecting guests; all their friends and kinsmen were at home, welcoming the Sabbath behind their own locked shutters. An unexpected knock at the door could mean only one thing to Marranos.

Mother and the children looked at Father, wondering if he were going to order them to flee, but he only nodded calmly to Raphael, one of the servants.

'We must not refuse to open the door,' he said, 'for that would invite suspicion. You must let them in, whoever they are. But not too quickly. Delay them as long as you can.'

After Raphael had left the room, Mother clutched with shaking hands at the silken cloth, embroidered with Hebrew letters and a gold Star of David, that covered the two plaited Sabbath loaves.

'We must hide everything,' she cried, 'or we're lost. We'll be caught red-handed, in the midst of all our Sabbath rituals, and how shall we be able to deny anything then? They'll send us back to Portugal, just as they sent that man in Bristol . . . Joachim Gunz . . . do you remember? My God, they'll send us back to the Inquisition, and then they'll . . .'

Father, who with the children's help was bundling the prayerbooks together, looked almost angry.

'Gracia,' he said, 'you are forgetting your dignity as the mistress of this house.'

'Dignity? For God's sake, let us hurry . . .'

'It is too late. We are in God's hands now.'

Robin looked up, startled, to see a man standing in the

doorway. For the past few moments he had been feeling a terrible guilt. He had wished he were not Jewish so that he might be free to join the players, and now he was being punished for it, together with his family. Then he saw the visitor's face, and thought he must be dreaming.

'The gentleman says he is a good friend to Master Robin,' announced Raphael.

'Your pardon, my masters,' said Will Shakespeare before anyone could speak, 'but I have come to return Robin's handkerchief, which he left in the theatre this afternoon. I got your address from Richard Lucy, Robin, but I hope I am not intruding . . .' His voice died away as his eyes took in the table set for the Sabbath meal; the festive clothes; the ceremonial wine; the plaited loaves; the candles; the embroidered cloth clutched in Mother's fingers, and the Hebrew prayerbooks which Philip had dropped on the floor and was now kissing apologetically, and a look of slow realization came over his face.

'I thank you, Master Shâkespeare, but you have come at an inopportune time,' said Father, his voice quite calm.

'So I see. Your servant wanted to take the handkerchief from me at the door, but I insisted on coming in. Of course, I didn't know . . .'

'But you know now, Master Shakespeare. As you see, we are Jews. Not New Christians, not converts, but genuine, practising Jews. We keep our religion as well as we can, though it is forbidden in this realm, and we live very close to death. And now are you going to do your duty, and hand us over to the Inquisition? It seems a great price to pay for a handkerchief.'

Master Shakespeare looked down at the small square of cambric in his hand, and then laughed.

'I must confess, Master Fernandez, that the handkerchief was just an excuse. I had to find some means of meeting you.

I wanted to persuade you to let Robin join our Company. The boy has real talent, and . . .'

'Master Shakespeare, my son does not need to act in your theatre,' Father interrupted. 'As a secret Jew he is acting a part all his life.'

'But you have such a bad opinion of us,' Will Shakespeare went on, 'and I had come to persuade you that you are mistaken. Robin tells me that you call us players "tinselled vagabonds", but that is not true. Why, my colleague John Heminges lives in a fine house in St Mary Aldermanbury, and he has fourteen children and cushions striped with silver. How can you call a man a vagabond who has silver-striped cushions in his house?'

Father looked at Will Shakespeare and then smiled, and Mother – who had been sitting with her hand clasped to her mouth as if to hold back a scream – relaxed a little.

'No doubt you have the same false opinion of us Jews as I have of you players,' said Father. 'Now, Master Shakespeare, an important choice lies before you. Are you going to betray us to the authorities or are you going to join us at supper?'

Will Shakespeare paused for a moment, and then took his seat at the table.

Chapter Six

Will Shakespeare did not betray the Fernandez family, and life at St Olave's continued much as usual, except that – for Robin, at least – there was a great deal more excitement.

Now that he was a protégé of the Lord Chamberlain's Men, every season seemed to hold some new marvel. Sometimes it was an invitation to sing in a masque or at a wedding feast in some rich man's house; at other times he appeared as a chorister in a new stage play. Father grumbled continuously at the amount of school work he was missing, but Master Breakstaff was less concerned. The school was used to having its scholars snatched away to take part in entertainments; besides, Robin worked hard at his lessons in the evenings.

Philip was envious, and Frances never stopped wishing she had been born a boy. Her marriage to Thomas Mendes had been fixed for the following summer, and not even the sumptuous satins and velvets that were being bought for her trousseau brought her much consolation.

'If only Thomas were more like Romeo!' she sighed. 'If only *he* spoke such beautiful poetry! But he never opens his silly mouth, except to put food in it.'

'You ought to hire Will Shakespeare to write his lines,' said Robin, but Frances only glared at him and muttered that some people had been born lucky and should be grateful for it.

But it was not only his theatrical activities that made Robin so glad to be alive. As the year wore on, all three children discovered that life in London was full of enchantment, and they wondered how they could ever have thought Bristol a fine city. In London there were pageants, and firework displays and water games on the Thames, and Guild processions ablaze with banners. There were visits to tournaments and to tilt-yard shows to see knights in shining armour riding in carriages that seemed to move of their own accord, visits to the zoo at the Tower, where one could peer through wooden lattices at four lions, a tiger and a porcupine. There was Bartholomew Fair, where the side-shows and monsters and jugglers and fire-eaters were more spectacular than those at any fair in Bristol, the gingerbread sweeter, the fat women fatter, and the ballad-singers and minstrels more melodious.

There were other entertainments too, but the children did their best to avoid these. People loved watching the beggars being whipped through the streets, branded or put in the stocks, and one could also visit Bethlehem, the lunatic asylum, to see the poor madmen lying chained and howling on their beds of straw. But public executions were the most popular entertainment of all; Richard Lucy never missed one if he could help it, and he always insisted on giving Robin the details.

'I saw such a fine spectacle this morning,' he would say. 'The fellow who was being hanged was a highwayman . . .

he wore crimson taffeta breeches, and he made such a witty speech from the gallows. The crowd laughed and cheered – it was better than going to the play. You were a fool to miss it, Robin. But I must be home to my dinner now – all that excitement has given me an appetite.'

Richard could sing as sweetly as an angel, and he wrote poems about flowers, nightingales and lovely ladies, yet he enjoyed nothing so much as a bloody execution or – failing that – a visit to a cock-fight or bear-baiting. Robin could not understand it. Sometimes he wondered why he and Richard were friends. At other times he wondered if *he* were the one who was not quite normal. Then it occurred to him that Will Shakespeare hated bear-baitings and probably hated executions too, and he felt comforted.

All this time Robin saw very little of Dr Lopez, except when he glimpsed him in synagogue during the Jewish New Year and Day of Atonement services.

These two festivals were the high point of the Jewish religious year, and were known as the High Holydays. They were really one festival, for Rosh Hashana, the New Year, inaugurated a ten-day period of prayer and repentance which culminated in the solemn fast of Yom Kippur, the Day of Atonement. During Rosh Hashana Jews ate honey-cakes and apples dipped in honey to symbolize their hope of a sweet year to come, but on Yom Kippur they ate and drank nothing at all. And while they prayed and repented of their sins of the past year, God sat hunched in Heaven over two mighty books, inscribing in one the names of all those people who were destined to die during the coming year, and in the other the names of those who would live.

Yom Kippur began at sunset with a prayer called Kol Nidre, which meant 'all vows', and which many people believed had been composed for the benefit of the Marranos. It asked God to ignore any vows the people might make under duress, such as the vows of forced conversion to another faith.

For schoolboys like Robin and Philip these holy festivals were difficult to observe, for they had to go to school as usual in order to avert suspicion. Being under the age of thirteen they did not have to fast on Yom Kippur. But even so, it was hard to laugh and scuffle with their schoolmates, or wrestle with Latin and algebra, or recite Christian prayers, or tremble before Master Breakstaff, on a day when all the Jews in the world were trembling, either openly or secretly, before God.

Not until the day's lessons were over were they able to hurry to the synagogue, where the long litany was drawing to a close. All the adults – the men in their white prayer-shawls, and the shadowy figures of the women behind the grille that separated the sexes – looked tired and pale after the day's praying and fasting. But before they hurried home to a well-earned festive meal, there was one more ritual that had to be observed. The Rosh Hashana and Yom Kippur services should have ended with a long-drawn-out piercing blast on the Shofar, which was a kind of trumpet fashioned from a ram's horn. For Marranos, who had to pray without being overheard, this was impossible, so the Shofar was merely lifted symbolically to the Rabbi's lips.

In Portugal and Spain, Father told the children, Marranos had dealt with this problem by riding out to some empty valley or lonely mountain-top, and there blowing the Shofar where its sound would not reach prying ears. Now, as the Rabbi of St Olave's pretended to blow on the great curving horn, Robin imagined he could hear its music reverberating over distant hills

Meanwhile Robin's theatrical activities were keeping him busy, and there were his lessons to attend to whenever he had an hour or so to spare.

69

'Do you want to know a secret?' asked Richard. 'I had it from Nicholas Tooley, and he said I might tell you.'

He and Robin were on their way from rehearsal for a new play at the Rose Theatre. It was New Year's Day – January the 1st 1594 – and as Robin looked across the grey waters of the Thames and saw the steely spires of London clustered against the leaden sky he thought happily of the year that lay before him – another year of the music and masques and plays and all the wonders and marvels of the capital.

'What will you give me if I tell you?' Richard went on.

'I'll buy you an almond tart when we get to Cheapside.'

'An almond tart *and* a piece of marchpane.'

'All right then. Now tell me.'

Richard drew a deep breath and paused for a moment. Then he said, 'We're going to sing at a banquet in Lord Essex's house.'

'*What?*'

'It's true. Master Burbage told Nicholas, and Nicholas told me. My Lord of Essex is having guests from the North to stay with him, and there is to be a feast in their honour at Essex House, and *we* are to provide the music. It's next month, the third of February, and rehearsals start after Twelfth Night.'

Robin gazed at him, his eyes shining. There had been entertainments over the Twelve Days of Christmas, and he had taken part in some of them, but to sing at Essex House, and to have the great Earl himself, the Queen's favourite, as his host . . . why, there was nowhere higher he could climb, except perhaps . . .

'After that, maybe, we shall be invited to perform before the Queen herself,' said Richard, answering what was in Robin's mind, and the two boys hugged each other gleefully.

They were walking home across London Bridge, since the river was too icy and choppy for the boats, and although it was a long walk it was an interesting one. The Bridge was the most important street in London. It was lined on either side by some of the finest shops and houses in the city, and it was covered along its entire length by a roof-like structure, so that one could walk right across the Thames on a rainy day without getting wet.

'The people who live here are lucky,' sighed Richard. 'They can throw all their rubbish into the river and not have it piling up in the streets. Yesterday my mother came out of our house and stepped right into a pile of chicken entrails . . . *and* she was going visiting in her best white satin shoes.'

Although Robin always enjoyed walking across the Bridge, there was one part of it which he hated. This was the great stone gate and tower at the Southwark end, where the heads of executed traitors were displayed on poles as a dreadful warning. Though Robin tried to look jaunty whenever he passed this particular place, the heads always made him shiver. There were at least thirty of them on this New Year's Day, and they looked like rotten apples as they rattled in the chill January wind, staring with their empty eye-sockets across the gleaming river.

'Do you have heads like this on your bridge in Bristol?' asked Richard.

Robin admitted that there were no heads on the Avon bridge, and secretly he was glad of it.

Richard picked up a stone and hurled it high into the air, and it struck one of the heads, which tumbled from its pole and fell into the river with a great splash.

'You'll get into trouble for that,' gasped Robin, half expecting to see a constable suddenly appear and haul Richard away.

'I didn't mean to knock it down,' said Richard. 'Come on, let's run.'

He and Robin linked hands and set off at a breathless trot, not stopping till they arrived at the place where Nonsuch House soared above the middle drawbridge – a splendid

71

building four storeys high, painted green and white, and crowned with copper-plated towers and onion-shaped domes. But even while they stood and admired its glittering expanse of glass windows and its gilded panels and weather-vane, Robin could not help thinking of the great stone gate near the Southwark shore. In his mind he still saw the cluster of poles, and the sightless heads watching him.

Robin had looked forward to coming home to a good supper and the warmth of firelight and candlelight. But when he arrived at St Olave's, he realized at once that something was very wrong.

As soon as he came into the great chamber he saw that his parents had a guest, and that the visit was not a happy one. It was Dunstan Ames, leader of the Marrano community of London, purveyor of groceries to the Queen's Household, and Dr Lopez's father-in-law, who sat there, a goblet of wine untouched on the table before him, and his face very grave. Father and Mother were also looking pale and shaken.

Robin took off his cap and bowed politely to the guest, and then made to leave the room, but Father called him back.

'Stay, Robin, I think you should hear this news. You will hear it soon enough in any case, and Dr Lopez has always been especially kind to you.'

'Dr Lopez?' asked Robin quickly, feeling a sudden icy shiver in his spine. 'Has anything happened to him?'

'He has been arrested,' said Dunstan Ames. 'A troop of soldiers called at his home this morning and took him into custody at Essex House. They did not say what the charge was. My daughter is distraught. She tells me they ransacked the house from top to bottom, searching for God knows what, but apparently could find nothing.'

'Essex House?' said Robin, thinking of the invitation he had received, and the noble Earl who had once been Dr

Lopez's friend. 'Do you mean it was Lord Essex who had Dr Lopez arrested?'

'Apparently it was.'

'But it was also Lord Essex who arrested Signor Ferreira, and so . . .'

'What do *you* know about Signor Ferreira?' asked Master Ames sternly, and Robin suddenly realized that his parents were staring at him in amazement.

There was nothing he could do now except tell the secret he had kept for so many months. 'Dr Lopez made Philip and Frances and me promise not to tell anyone . . . not even our parents,' he concluded, 'but now *you* know, sir, and so we can't keep silent any longer.'

'Indeed not,' replied Father. 'You are to be admired for keeping your counsel for so long. I must say I'm surprised at Frances – I've never know *her* keep a secret before.'

'But I still don't quite understand,' interrupted Mother. 'Do you mean that Dr Lopez has been *pretending* to be in the pay of Spain so that he might more easily obtain information of use to this country?'

'Exactly, my dear,' replied Master Ames. 'Of course, we always knew it was a dangerous game he was playing. My poor daughter worried about it night and day. She would have preferred him not to meddle in State Affairs. But, you see, it was at the special request of the late Secretary of State that he did it.'

'Sir Francis Walsingham, I know,' Robin broke in, feeling pleased now at being included in a serious adult discussion.

'And does the Queen know about it?' asked Mother.

'Sir Francis felt it was wiser to keep this little matter a secret between my son-in-law and himself,' replied Master Ames.

'Then nobody else knows?'

'Nobody at all. Except my daughter and us, of course.'

'But . . .' Mother faltered. Robin saw a little frown creep

73

between her eyebrows, and suddenly a terrible thought came into his mind and he also knew it to be in the minds of all the others.

Walsingham was the only one of all the Queen's Counsellors who knew that Dr Lopez was *pretending* to be a traitor for England's sake. Walsingham was the only person who could prove his innocence without a doubt. *And Walsingham was dead.*

Chapter Seven

Robin went to visit Mistress Lopez a few days later, and found her rather calmer than he had expected.

'There is nothing they can accuse my husband of . . . nothing that any sane man would believe,' she said. 'They searched our house and found nothing. The Lord Treasurer, his brother Sir Robert Cecil and my Lord of Essex all examined my husband, and he gave a satisfactory answer to every one of their questions. They tried to trap him, but they could not. The Cecils are sure that Lord Essex is mistaken . . . they are convinced of my husband's innocence. Dr Nunez told me all this, and he had it from Sir Robert Cecil himself.'

Robin was suitably impressed. He already knew that Hector Nunez was in the confidence of the Queen's ministers, and kept them supplied with secret information from Spain and Portugal.

'Then, if the Cecils believe Dr Lopez to be innocent . . .' he began.

'Not only the Cecils. My husband has a more powerful ally than they.' Mistress Lopez drew herself up to her full height, and spoke with dignity. 'The Queen herself knows him to be innocent, and she told Lord Essex so.'

'She *told* Lord Essex?' gasped Robin. 'Then surely, Madam, there is nothing to fear.'

'Nothing at all to fear. Master Nunez heard it all from Sir Robert. It seems that while he was speaking with the Queen on this same matter, Lord Essex came into the audience-chamber, whereupon the Queen turned on him in a great rage. She called him a rash, temerarious youth, and accused him of bringing false charges against my husband. She said she was much displeased . . . that her honour was at stake . . . that she knew quite well that the poor man was innocent. Lord Essex turned first red and then white, Dr Nunez said, and then the Queen dismissed him from her presence, and he ran out of the room like a whipped cur and has not been seen at Court since.'

Robin felt as if a great load of anxiety had been lifted from him.

'Then everything *must* be well,' he cried. 'You have nothing to fear, believe me, madam. Nothing can harm Dr Lopez if the Queen is on his side.'

'I know, I know. But what I don't understand is why anyone should *want* to harm him. Lord Essex was always such a pleasant young man. And my husband has never done him anything but good . . . he has done nothing but good all his life. He cured Lord Leicester of the toothache; he even saved the Queen's life, when she was ill with the ague. He has always been loved and honoured. Why should evil men plot against him now, in his old age?'

In spite of the hopeful news she had just given Robin,

76

Mistress Lopez's eyes filled with tears. She walked to the window and looked out sadly at the garden, its orchard trees thin and leafless now, and the healing plants of the herb garden hidden under the January snow.

Rehearsals for the recital at Essex House began next day, and poor Dr Lopez and his troubles were once more relegated to the back of Robin's mind. To his great joy, Philip was also chosen to be a chorister, for his voice had greatly improved during the past year.

'So now I shall have *two* of them neglecting their lessons to go caterwauling in high places,' thundered Father, though secretly he was proud of both his sons. 'I can only thank God my third child is a girl, and obliged to stay discreetly at home.' Frances said nothing, but stole away to her bedchamber and cried with frustration.

Meanwhile, there was no news of Dr Lopez. Robin expected every day to hear that he had been released, but nothing happened. When he called to see Mistress Lopez, he found her more worried than she had been during his previous visit.

'I had thought he would be home by now,' she said, and the hand with which she was pouring a goblet of wine for Robin trembled. 'The Queen believes him innocent, and so does the Lord Treasurer, so why are they still keeping him?'

'Has Dr Nunez heard nothing?' asked Robin, feeling a certain glow of importance at being so close to State secrets.

'Nothing at all. Sir Robert Cecil has kept remarkably silent of late. All we know is that my husband is still confined at Essex House.'

When, later that day, Robin told his brother about his conversation with Mistress Lopez, Philip gazed at him wide-eyed and said, 'But we're going to Essex House next week. For the recital.'

'And what of it,' asked Robin, putting on his most pompous big-brother voice.

'We might see Dr Lopez there.'

Robin shook with laughter.

'Idiot!' he said, as soon as he could speak. 'Do you suppose he will be sitting at table among the guests? Or singing in the choir with us, maybe?'

'I thought we might meet him in a corridor, or on the stairs,' said Philip, abashed.

'That's unlikely. They're probably keeping him chained up in a dungeon. Or locked in one of the rooms. After all, Essex House is a big place. I shouldn't be surprised if it isn't twice as big as our house. It might even be twice as big as Master Mendes's house.'

Philip could not reply, so overwhelmed was he at the thought of so much magnificence.

Essex House was more than twice as big as Master Mendes's house. Built around a quadrangle, it faced on to the Strand and had splendid gardens and orchards sweeping down to the frozen Thames. As the chilly choristers stepped out of the night into a blaze of candles and torches, exquisite carvings and gold-threaded tapestries, they almost felt that they had come to one of the Royal palaces by mistake, and that they would be ushered at any moment into the Queen's presence.

And yet it was not the Queen who greeted them after all, but a young man, handsome as a god and tall as a giant, with thick auburn hair cascading over his shoulders. He wore a doublet of white velvet embroidered with silver and a matching cloak lined with peacock satin, and was in every way a most imposing figure. This was the mighty Earl of Essex himself, come down into the vestibule to welcome his choristers as if they had been great lords and not nervous little boys whose throats were already beginning to feel scratchy.

Robin could scarcely believe his eyes. This was the man who was plotting against Dr Lopez; Robin had envisaged someone with a sly face and cruel eyes, not this charming gallant with eyes as merry as Will Shakespeare's and a laugh that made the wainscoting ring.

'They say the Queen is in love with him,' whispered Richard Lucy as the Earl's secretary ushered the boys upstairs to the tiring-room, where they were to change into their matching scarlet doublets and white ruffs.

'She *can't* be,' replied Philip indignantly. 'She's much older than he is.'

Having clattered up the great staircase, past the carved beasts that glared at them from the pillars of the balustrade, the boys found themselves on a wide landing surrounded on three sides by doors, all just as intricately carved. The solitary door on the right-hand side was slightly ajar, and from it spilled a dazzling light and the sound of musicians tuning their instruments.

'That is the great chamber, where the banquet is to be held,' said Master Forsham, the Earl's secretary, who was a pale young man with an earnest face and a slight stammer. 'Beyond it lies the long gallery, where the company will dance after supper. These other doors lead to the bedchambers.' Then seeing Philip examining the carving on one of the doors, he leaped forward, grasped the boy's wrist, and said quickly, 'No, not in there, lad. *That* door leads to the Earl's own apartment. Come, I will show you where your tiring-room is. You will find soap and warm water, and saffron cakes and ale to refresh you before you sing.'

As he allowed himself to be led towards the tiring-room, Philip began to wonder why Master Forsham had been so eager to pull him away from the Earl's door.

It's only a bedchamber after all, he thought. Just a room with a bed in it. Is there some dread secret about it? Does the Earl keep a dragon there? And then something occurred to him, and he stood still, his mouth wide open in sudden surmise.

Was it possible that Dr Lopez was being kept prisoner in the Earl's bedchamber, just a short distance away from the feasting and dancing and the music of lutes and violins and hautboys?

Robin was also thinking about Dr Lopez as the choristers sang madrigals and watched the Earl and his guests munching their way through a marvellous banquet.

Before him was a spectacle richer than anything he had ever dreamed of. The great chamber was about a hundred feet long, its ceiling and chimney-piece exquisitely patterned and its walls hung not only with the traditional tapestries but also with paintings in gold frames. There was stained glass, coloured like jewels, in the windows; the long table was laid with knives and vessels of solid gold and silver, and each guest had one of the new-fangled forks in addition to his knife and spoon.

The guests themselves were so magnificently attired that one might easily have taken them to be characters out of one of Will Shakespeare's plays. Such lavish displays of brilliant satin, velvet and gold embroidery belonged on the stage of a theatre rather than a private house, Robin thought. And yet, somewhere behind all this fairy-tale splendour, the music and feasting and the pure bird-like voices of the choristers, there lurked a dark shadow. Somewhere in this great house Dr Lopez was being held prisoner . . . being tortured and terrorized, perhaps . . . while some cunning plot was devised for his downfall.

Now Richard Lucy's clear soprano voice rose into the perfumed air.

'Diaphena, like the daffodowndilly,' he sang.
'White as the sun, fair as the lily,
Heigh-ho, how I do love thee!
I do love thee as my lambs
Are beloved of their dams;
How blessed were I if thou wouldst prove me!'

At the long table the mouths went on munching as the procession of livery-clad ushers and gentlemen-in-waiting came and went, bringing in one sumptuous course after another. There was a boar's head so fierce that the boys trembled at the sight of it, and a roast peacock still clad in all his finery of brilliant feathers; cygnets and cranes and a whole silent choir of singing-birds. There were gleaming fish swimming on seas of parsley, and salads decorated with flowers. Best of all, there was a great array of pies and tarts, jellies and candied fruits, custards and syllabubs. And last of all came the climax of the banquet . . . a procession of gold platters bearing subtleties made of sugar and gilded march-pane. The last and most splendid of all was a replica of Essex House, complete down to the last sugared turret. This subtlety drew applause even from the Earl's pampered guests, and Robin thought it would be a pity to eat it.

But eaten it was; then the guests rinsed their greasy hands in rosewater and retired to the gallery to dance or dice or play at cards, leaving the hungry choristers and ushers to sit down to the remains of the feast. Strangely enough, there seemed to be almost as much food left on the table as there had been at the beginning of the evening.

'My Lord Essex must be very rich,' observed Philip. 'He must be almost as rich as the Queen.'

Robin was too busy trying to balance a piece of stuffed carp on the end of his fork to reply. After the sauce had dripped down his sleeve and the fish had fallen off three times, he finally gave up and used his fingers instead.

Philip had said nothing to his brother about his suspicion that Dr Lopez might be locked in the Earl's bedroom. Now, as he ate, and listened to the music of the dance as it drifted through the half-open door that led to the gallery, a plan came into his mind, and he said nothing about *that* to Robin either.

It was not that he was afraid of being overheard by one of the other choristers. It was simply that he did not want Robin to know anything of the wild scheme that was in his head.

During all the ten years of his life, Philip had suffered from being the younger son. It was Robin who was the centre of all Father's hopes and plans; Robin who sang and acted with the Lord Chamberlain's Men; Robin who was the friend and confidant of Dr Lopez and Will Shakespeare, and all that Philip could ever do was stand silently in Robin's shadow. It was not quite as bad as being a girl, but it was bad enough.

So now it was time for a change. Philip, who had followed all his life, was going to take the lead. He was going to find Dr Lopez. He would find him entirely on his own, and Robin would know nothing about it till the deed had been done.

There was no time to be lost. Philip's plan was ripe, and he must act now, before his courage deserted him. He put down his knife and spoon, clutched at the place where he imagined his heart to be, and muttered, 'I feel sick.'

Robin stopped chewing and looked at him. 'You're not going to be ill, are you?' he asked, not altogether kindly.

'I'm ill already.'

'You don't look ill. You've eaten too much, that's all.'

'I've a terrible pain in my stomach,' said Philip indignantly. Then, seeing that Robin looked unimpressed, he uttered a loud groan.

It worked. Robin at last seemed concerned; the other

choristers glanced up from their food and stared, and Master Forsham came running to ask what was wrong.

'I feel dizzy, and my stomach aches,' moaned Philip. 'Could I please go to the tiring-room and lie down?'

'I'll send for a physician at once,' babbled the poor secretary anxiously.

'N-no, please, I don't want a physician,' said Philip quickly. 'I've eaten too much, that's all.'

'A spider boiled in wine is an excellent cure for the stomach ache. We have plenty of spiders in the kitchen – I could ask one of the servants . . .'

'It's very kind of you, sir, but I'm sure I would soon feel better if I could lie down for a while,' gulped Philip, who was beginning to feel genuinely ill now.

'Come then, I'll take you to the tiring-room. Lean on me, poor lad.' And Philip, who had hoped to be allowed to leave the chamber without fuss, had to submit to being put to bed in the tiring-room by the Earl's nervous secretary.

After Master Forsham had gone back to the great chamber, Philip waited for a few minutes and then crept out of bed and back into the corridor. The Earl's door faced him, dark and secretive in the wavering torchlight. Was Dr Lopez *really* a prisoner behind its noble carvings? And if Philip *did* find him, what in God's name would happen next? And why had his knees turned to jelly? And what would happen if somebody caught him?

Philip swallowed hard, and then tapped nervously at the door. There was no reply. The door stared back at him blankly.

'He couldn't have heard me,' thought Philip, and tapped again, much louder this time. Again there was silence. All he could hear was the distant trilling of recorders and hautboys, and something else – a kind of steady, insistent thumping sound . . . drums? The dancers carousing in the long gallery?

It was a few moments before Philip realized that the sound was the beating of his own heart.

He twisted the door-handle, expecting to find the door locked, and was surprised and a little scared when it suddenly swung open. He looked back fearfully to see if anyone was watching, but the corridor was still deserted. Summoning up all his courage, he crept into the Earl's bedchamber and closed the door after him.

To his secret relief, the room was empty. It was also the most sumptuous bedchamber he had ever seen. The blazing logs in the fireplace dimly illuminated a massive four-poster bed hung with gold-embroidered satin, chests and cabinets and a great desk inlaid with coloured wood, window-seats piled high with velvet cushions, silver basins and ewers and a huge silver-framed mirror. There was a 'posy' carved above the chimney-piece; Philip approached, and in the flickering firelight could just make out the words:

> Hast thou a friend as heart may wish at will?
> Then use him so to have his friendship still.

Reading this, Philip felt strangely comforted. If Lord Essex valued friendship so highly, he thought, then surely he would do nothing to harm an old man who had always been his good friend.

This new feeling of reassurance did not last long. Suddenly Philip heard footsteps in the corridor, and then the door-handle began to turn. Without stopping to think, he leaped into the great bed and pulled the curtains close. And only just in time, too . . . Peering fearfully through a chink in the heavy satin, he saw Master Forsham glide into the room and close the door carefully behind him. First he lit the candles, and the shadowy room sprang into vivid life and colour. Next he seated himself at the desk, unlocked it, and took out a sheaf of documents and some writing vellum, which he spread out on the lid before him. Then he began to write,

84

stopping at intervals to consult the documents, or to sprinkle sand on something he had written.

Philip groaned inwardly. It had never occurred to him that the Earl's secretary might leave the festivities and come here to catch up with his correspondence. Suppose he were to stay all evening, until the Earl came to bed, and Philip were never able to make his escape and rejoin the other choristers . . . The boy's spine prickled with terror at the thought. To make matters worse, he wanted to sneeze. He would be caught . . . he would be executed as a spy, and his head would join the grisly array at the Southwark end of London Bridge.

Much as he struggled to keep back the threatening sneeze, it came at last. 'Ah . . . ah . . . ker . . . chew!' he bellowed, so loudly that it seemed the mythological figures on the bed-curtains must clap their hands over their ears in dismay.

Philip shut his eyes and waited, trembling, for the curtains to be pulled aside and for Master Forsham to drag him out of his hiding-place. But nothing happened, except that Philip imagined for a moment that he could hear someone moaning as if in fear. He peered between the curtains again, just in time to see the Earl's secretary scuttling out of the room as if evil spirits were at his heels. He rushed out into the corridor, and the door slammed after him.

Philip did not stop to wonder why Master Forsham was so frightened. It was enough that he was miraculously free. He jumped out of the bed and made for the door. But as he passed the desk he noticed that the secretary had left a pile of documents lying there in disarray, and his curiosity got the better of him. He skimmed quickly through the papers, which were mainly written in Latin. Then, suddenly, his heart missed a beat. The last paper was in English, and the name 'Lopez' leaped up at him from the crackling parchment.

There was no time to read it. If he lingered, Master Forsham might come back and catch him red-handed. Philip thrust the paper down the front of his doublet and crept out into the corridor. He was now both a spy *and* a thief, he thought, but his sins would weigh lightly on him if they helped to save Dr Lopez.

In the long gallery the guests were dancing the lavolta, the gentlemen lifting their partners high into the air as if they weighed no more than thistledown. With each leap the ladies' vast wired skirts fluttered like the wings of giant butterflies, and their shrieks of laughter rang out above the music of the flutes and virginals.

Philip searched about anxiously until he found Robin. He wanted to go home before he betrayed himself; the stolen document inside his doublet prickled as if it were on fire. But Robin was enjoying the music, the merriment, the great tapestry of shifting patterns and colours, and he was in no hurry to leave.

'I still don't feel well,' poor Philip persisted. 'I know I ought to be at home in bed.'

'You *look* quite well,' said Robin unsympathetically. 'And we can't leave early, we don't get invited to an Earl's house every day, do we?'

Thank God for that, Philip thought, but before he could say any more he saw, to his horror, Lord Essex himself push his way through the revellers towards the place where he and Robin stood.

The Earl smiled at the boys, but it seemed to Philip that those keen eyes were boring right through the scarlet velvet of his doublet to the place where the document lay hidden. Did he know it was missing? Did he suspect Philip? And what had happened to Master Forsham? He was not to be seen anywhere.

'My secretary tells me you have been ill,' said the Earl pleasantly. 'But I see you are quite recovered?'

86

'Thank you, yes, my lord,' Philip stammered. 'I . . . I think the excitement was too much for me.'

'Or the sweetmeats, perhaps?' The Earl's mouth twitched with amusement.

Philip blushed, and Robin piped up, 'I told him so, my lord, but he insists that he ate practically nothing.'

'Well eating too much is not so great a fault as drinking too much,' said the Earl drily. 'I fear my secretary, Master Forsham, must have had one tankard too many this evening. He swears he met a hobgoblin in my bedchamber not half an hour ago. In *my* bedchamber, where I have slept peacefully all these years without ever encountering any unwelcome guests, apart from the occasional flea . . .'

'W-what did it look like, sir?' asked Philip, his voice trembling.

'He didn't see it clearly. He says he heard it sneeze . . . it had, it seems, a terrifying sneeze, a sound straight out of Hell. And then he saw two red eyes, like burning coals, staring at him, and he turned and fled.' The Earl saw Philip staring at him in dismay, and his face softened. 'Don't be afraid, my boy,' he said kindly. 'Essex House is not haunted, to my knowledge. Master Forsham is a nervous gentleman . . . this is not the first time he has seen visitations from another world. But I dare say you and your brother are more sensible.'

'Y-yes, sir,' quavered Philip, feeling his heart sink. It was obvious that he and Robin must now stay till the end of the evening; to leave early would look like cowardice. But he must not dance for fear the precious document might drop out of his breeches. He wished he had never longed to be a hero.

'Do you know what this paper is?' Father asked.

The boys had arrived home at last, and Philip had told his story. Father's first reaction had been anger; Philip, he declared, had put not only his own silly neck but those of the whole family in danger. 'But your motives were good ones, and your escape a miracle,' he added, more gently, 'and so I shall have to forgive you.' Robin said nothing, but he looked at Philip with amazement and what was obviously a new respect.

And now the boys were standing before the fire in the small dining-parlour while Father examined the document Philip had taken from the Earl's desk. His face was very grave, and the boys noticed that the hand which held the sheet of parchment was trembling.

'This paper is a signed confession,' he said at last.

'A confession?' gasped Robin. 'Not by Dr Lopez?'

'Not *by* him. *About* him, which is just as bad. This document is signed by one Esteban Ferreira, now a prisoner in the Tower . . .'

'But we know him,' interrupted Robin excitedly. 'We met him at Dr Lopez's house.'

'And we didn't like him,' added Philip. 'He had a sly face. And Dr Lopez was angry with him.'

'Is he the gentleman you told me about?' asked Father. 'The one who lodged with Dr Lopez, and was later arrested?' The boys nodded, and Father went on, 'It seems, then, that he has not repaid the doctor's hospitality with any great goodwill.'

'What does the confession say, sir?' asked Robin, feeling a sudden tightening in his throat.

'The worst, I fear. Signor Ferreira admits here that Dr Lopez had promised to poison our Lady the Queen.'

Poison! The boys stared at one another, remembering the healing herbs in the garden at Holborn, and Dr Lopez saying, 'Her Majesty is graciously pleased to number me among her friends. She even wears a ruby ring I once gave her.' Poison? No, it was not true; it could not possibly be true.

'Dr Lopez was in the pay of Philip of Spain,' Father's voice went on relentlessly. 'Dr Lopez promised the king that he would be the Queen's executioner – the method to be poison. Signor Ferreira says so in his confession.'

'Then Signor Ferreira is lying,' Robin burst out angrily.

'Very likely,' replied Father wearily. 'Most confessions are obtained under torture – didn't you know that? Who knows what a man might confess to when he is on the rack? The signature is shaky, and that seems suspicious. See for yourself.' He held out the paper to the boys, and they stared at the scrawled 'Esteban Ferreira'. The letters were faint and cramped, as if they were half-dead with pain

There was a long silence, and then Robin asked, 'What shall we do, sir?'

Father looked back at him, and smiled.

'Without this confession, the doctor's enemies will find it difficult to condemn him,' he said. 'So we shall send it where they cannot find it.'

'You mean destroy it?' gasped Philip.

'God forgive me for sinning against Her Majesty's officers,' replied Father, 'but I feel I have a duty to save our friend . . . particularly since I suspect that he is innocent.'

He walked towards the chimney-piece and dropped the paper in the fire, and he and the boys watched as it caught the flames and crumbled away into ashes.

Chapter Eight

For the next three days the Fernandez family lived in fear, thinking of the ashes in the grate, and wondering if Philip's escapade in Essex House had been discovered. But as time passed without the expected accusing knock on the door, they began to relax and feel themselves safe at last.

Then, on the fourth day, the knock came, just as the family were seated at dinner.

'They've found out,' gulped Philip. 'They've come to arrest me. Oh, what shall I do?' and he dropped his spoon and tried to clamber under the table.

'Will you give us all away, ninny?' cried Father, hauling Philip back on to his chair and replacing the greasy spoon in his shaking fingers. 'You must stay and face them, and act a better part than you have ever played before. God knows you get enough practice in that vile theatre of yours.'

But the unexpected visitors were not, after all, the emissaries of the Earl of Essex. The figure that appeared a few moments later in the doorway, looking stern and sad, was Dunstan Ames. At his side was something the Fernandez family took at first to be a wandering beggar, so dirty, weary and bedraggled did it look. Examining this dismal creature, Robin saw that it was a boy, taller and somewhat older than himself. Although his clothes seemed to be of good quality, they were torn with brambles and splashed with mud, and the fine boots were also mud-caked, split and gaping at the toes. The boy's dark hair was wet and tangled; his fingers frost-bitten, his face covered with grime, and he limped. In all his life, thought Robin, he had never seen such a wretched creature standing in his father's elegant dining-parlour.

'This is my grandson, Anthony Lopez,' said Dunstan Ames. 'I could have hoped your first meeting with him would be more propitious.'

The Fernandez family, too shocked to speak, could only gaze at the newcomer in disbelief. Of course they had heard about young Anthony from his proud parents. Robin had sometimes pictured him, a scholar at Winchester, as a younger edition of his father, learning to take his place one day in Court society. He had even envied him. What connection could there possibly be between *that* Anthony Lopez and this pathetic creature, who now looked back at him with an expression very like fear?

Dunstan Ames answered the question before anyone could ask it. 'He has run away from school,' he said. 'As soon as the news leaked through to Winchester that my son-in-law had been arrested, the boy's schoolmates and schoolmasters began to taunt and threaten him. Besides, he wanted to be with his mother at her time of need. So he ran away in the night, and set out to walk all the way to London. He arrived less than an hour ago . . .'

'But why have you brought him here, Master Ames?' asked Father. 'And in such a condition?'

91

'Because I fear he may be in danger as long as he remains in London. Those who are plotting against my son-in-law could well wish his innocent son out of the way as well. I am arranging to send him to my brother in Antwerp . . . I hope within a few days . . . but until that time the boy must be hidden, and where better than in your house?' Then, seeing Father looking puzzled, Master Ames added, 'If my Lord Essex seeks to arrest him, where else would his envoys search but in his mother's house, and then mine? A messenger from Winchester has already called there, and may well do so again. But you are not known to these gentlemen. You are newcomers to London, and none suspect that you are New Christians. If my Anthony can be safe anywhere, it must be with you.'

Father, looking dazed, could only politely murmur, 'He is welcome to stay as long as he chooses.' It was left to Mother to say what the rest of the family were thinking.

'How like a man,' she cried, 'to bring him to us still reeking from the journey! Why didn't you give the poor child some food, and wash him, and let him rest? Look at him! How could you be so cruel?'

Dunstan Ames smiled sadly.

'His mother wanted to do all those things,' he said, 'but I persuaded her to part with him at once, for his own sake.' Here Anthony's face crumpled as if he were about to cry, and Master Ames went on, 'You ladies are all the same – you put kindness before good sense. Think, Mistress Fernandez, was it not good sense to bring him here, where he can rest in safety?'

Mother did not bother to answer. Within a few moments she had sent for the servants, and soon young Anthony was soaking in a tub of hot, scented water, while one of the maids prepared food and another was set to warming a comfortable bed. Meanwhile, Mother sorted out some of

92

Robin's clothes, which proved – when Anthony attempted to struggle into them – to be too small.

'It's no use . . . he's much taller than Robin,' sighed Mother. 'Why didn't you bring us some of his clothes, Master Ames? Do you expect him to travel to Antwerp naked?'

'I shall go to my daughter's house at once, Madam, and collect all that he needs,' said Master Ames, more afraid, at that moment, of Mistress Fernandez than of the Earl of Essex, the headmaster of Winchester, and all the spies of the Inquisition.

Anthony Lopez looked quite different when the Fernandez children saw him again next day. Bathed, fed, rested, and dressed in the elegant blue velvet tunic that his grandfather had brought from Holborn, he looked more like a young Court gallant than the bedraggled fugitive who had first arrived in their house. But his face was still pale, and his eyes kept their haunted look.

There was no time for Robin and Philip to talk to their guest at breakfast. Master Breakstaff and his cane could not be kept waiting, and as soon as the boys had swallowed some bread and ale they had to run to school. For the first time Robin envied his sister, cooped up at home among the women and the household chores. *She* could at least spend some time with Anthony. She would persuade her mother that hospitality towards the stranger was as much a duty as churning butter or stitching cushions.

When Robin and Philip came home for dinner, they found their sister glowing with excitement.

'Anthony has been telling me how he walked to London,' she said. 'He's had a terrible time. He fell into a ditch, and somebody stole his purse, and a farmer set the dogs on him. But some people were kind. A woman gave him food, and a man gave him a ride on a haycart. I do like him. He's handsome, and he listens to everything I say, and he doesn't think girls are silly, and he likes me. He says I'm pretty.' Here Frances blushed deeply.

'He must be *mad*!' declared Philip.

'Shush,' said Robin, trying not to laugh. 'He's our prisoner. He depends on us. That's why he has to be polite to you.'

'He's polite because he has good manners,' replied Frances loftily, 'which is more than I can say of *some* people. Oh, I do wish I could marry *him* instead of Thomas Mendes!'

Over dinner, the boys were able to observe their guest's good manners for themselves, and to learn more about his last few days.

'It all started when one of the boys at school received a letter from home, telling how my father had been arrested by Lord Essex,' Anthony explained. 'Of course he told his friends. Then the whispers started. At first they just called my father "villain" and "traitor". But then it became "Jew". And then everything changed for me.'

'How changed?' asked Robin.

'I used to think they liked me. I had so many friends at Winchester. All of a sudden I had no friends at all. Everyone retreated from me, spoke of Christ-killers and ritual murders, threatened me with death, commended the Inquisition . . . Everyone, even the schoolmasters, who should have known better . . .'

'Was it easy to escape?' asked Philip eagerly.

'No, it was very hard. Their eyes seemed to be watching me all the time. They even watched me at meals, lest I should prove a poisoner like my father. I had to wait till they were all asleep. Then I knotted the sheets on my bed, lowered myself from the window, and escaped under cover of darkness. When it grew light I kept to the forest paths, knowing they would come seeking me on the highway. My grandfather tells me an envoy from Winchester did come to my

94

house, but my mother persuaded him she had not seen me. I don't understand why they went after me, seeing that they hate me so much.'

Here Frances pressed Anthony's hand consolingly, while Mother heaped more chicken pie on his plate. Father contented himself with asking, 'Do you know how your grandfather intends to send you to Antwerp?'

'I think he means to hire a boat and some oarsmen, and have me borne up the river towards the sea one dark night.'

'But won't it be dangerous?' asked Frances nervously.

'No more dangerous than staying here. But I would rather stay. I want to stay until my father is either condemned or freed. My mother needs me to look after her.'

'It's *you* who need *her*, my poor lamb,' murmured Mother. But she would not say so openly, for fear of hurting Anthony's feelings.

That night Anthony woke shrieking from a nightmare in which his father swung from a gallows while an exultant crowd shouted 'Jew! Jew!' The Fernandez family, aroused from their sleep by his screams, lay wide awake for long after Anthony, soothed by Mother and a draught of blackcurrant cordial, had drifted off again.

'Let us hope his grandfather takes him away soon,' said Father next morning. 'I am glad to be able to offer sanctuary to the poor lad, but this business is disturbing my family and putting us all at risk.'

The rest of the family did not agree entirely. Mother enjoyed cossetting Anthony, while Frances delighted in his company. She had never felt such close friendship for a boy before. But Robin was in two minds about their guest. Often, when he looked at him, he saw himself in Anthony's place. How could anyone foretell the future? thought Robin. Had Anthony Lopez, clever, rich and highly-placed, only son of the Queen's physician, ever dreamed that he would one day depend on the goodwill and charity of strangers?

But this uneasy time did not last long. Six days after Anthony's arrival, Dunstan Ames called at the house one morning to announce that his grandson would be leaving for Antwerp that night. There would be no moon. A boat had been hired and was now lying on a quayside in the shadow of the Tower, and half a dozen oarsmen had received heavy bribes. A faithful servant of the Ames household would accompany Anthony on his journey up the Thames, past Tilbury, and out across the North Sea to Antwerp, where his uncle lived.

Anthony's last day in the Fernandez household passed all too quickly. Before they knew it the moonless night had arrived, and with it came Mistress Lopez, who had walked through the frosty darkness from Holborn to say good-bye to her son. Anthony, already dressed for the journey in black velvet and a dark cloak and hood, flung himself into her arms while she tearfully explained that she had not been able to visit him sooner because spies of Lord Essex were watching her every move.

'Even as I left tonight, one of his accursed hirelings was lurking in the trees near the house,' she added. 'But I was determined to see my dear boy, and I had Grandfather with me to give me courage, so I ignored him, and did not even look back to see if he were following or not.'

'We threw him off the scent as we passed through Newgate,' said Dunstan Ames. 'The watchman, wise fellow, straight away locked the gate after us, and the villain was left gaping on the other side.' Here all the children laughed despite themselves, although Father seemed disturbed at the idea that the Earl's spies might have followed Mistress Lopez all the way to Hart Street. Mother and Frances, meanwhile, were busy packing Anthony's clothes and food for the journey and plying the guests with wine and saffron cake. But Mistress Lopez could not eat.

'A plague on all our old friends!' she cried at last. 'They have robbed me of my husband, and now they are taking away my only child!'

'What are they going to do to my father?' quavered Anthony, at last asking the question he had not dared ask before.

'We can only pray,' replied Mistress Lopez. 'God knows he is innocent. God will protect him.'

'But what of the Queen?' cried Anthony. 'She was Father's friend. She used to invite us to her Christmas revels. She even gave me a piece of marchpane once. Is *she* going to abandon him?'

'No, no,' replied his mother quickly. 'His innocence will surely be proved. One day we shall all be together again.'

But meanwhile it was time to part. Mistress Lopez, Mother and Frances bade Anthony a tearful farewell, hugging and kissing him again and again. Robin and Philip, together with Father and Dunstan Ames, did not need to say good-bye yet, as they were accompanying Anthony and the servant Will Carter to the quayside, where the boat was moored. Anthony himself seemed calm enough now that the time had come.

The moon was hidden, and the streets dark, apart from the occasional glimmer of light from an ill-fitting shutter and the glow of Will's lantern. Already snowflakes hung on the air, and it appeared all wise folk were in bed or huddled by their fires. No one seemed to be out of doors apart from Anthony and his escorts, their footsteps crackling on the icy ground as they made their way past St Olave's Church, dedicated to the patron saint of Norway, where the Fernandez family ostensibly worshipped on Sundays; down Seething Lane, and through the maze of narrow streets that led towards the sleeping river.

Shorn of the dazzling parade of boats that enlivened it by day, the Thames lay silent and forbidding, its darkness pierced by the occasional point of light from the houses on London Bridge. The boat hired by Dunstan Ames was lit by a solitary lantern. Six burly oarsmen watched in uneasy silence as Will Carter humped the pack containing Anthony's clothes into the boat, following this with a pouch carefully filled by Mistress Fernandez with bread and cheese, cake and a flagon of wine.

'At least you won't starve to death during the journey,' said Dunstan Ames, trying to smile.

'Grandfather,' said Anthony without any answering smile, 'will my uncle in Antwerp want me?'

'Want you? Of course he will. But he won't keep you long. Soon your father will be free, God willing, and you shall come home again.'

There was no further delay. Anthony quickly hugged his grandfather and friends, and jumped into the boat. It swayed underfoot, the lantern swinging like a pendulum as the rope was uncoiled. Then the oars rose and dipped, and the boat began to move from the shore.

Anthony stood looking back, a small, lonely figure that grew ever smaller. Soon those on the shore could no longer see him. Robin, oblivious of the snowflakes that now clustered thickly on his cloak, watched as the dwindling lantern, no more than a dot of light, passed Traitor's Gate and slowly moved towards the sea.

A week later, Dr Lopez was formally charged with plotting to poison the Queen, and was brought to trial on a charge of High Treason.

Robin and Philip could not believe the news when they heard it. How could any accusations possibly be brought against the doctor when the vital evidence was lying, a handful of ashes, at the bottom of their hearth? But Father soon disillusioned them. '*Anything* is possible if the State wills it,' he said, 'and for some reason that I cannot understand, the State has willed the destruction of our good friend.'

It was Mistress Lopez who told the boys exactly how the charge had come to be brought against her husband. They had gone to visit her during their dinner-break, running most of the way across fields, ankle-deep in January snow.

Mistress Lopez's face was almost as white as the fields, and her eyes were red and swollen with crying. She settled the boys in front of the fire with tankards of mulled wine, and then huddled as close as she could to the blazing logs, for although the room was warm she could not stop shivering.

'There were two of them,' she said. 'Signor Ferreira – may a plague fall on him for all the good dinners he has eaten in this house – and another scoundrel named Tinoco, also from Portugal. Both of them were involved in shady dealings, and to protect themselves they incriminated my husband. It was they . . . foul rogues . . . who testified that he was sworn to poison the Queen.'

'They *both* confessed?' asked Robin.

'Of course. They were both interrogated. Oh, they were up to no good . . . spies for Spain, I have no doubt. So, being threatened with the rack, they were both quick to admit that they were merely being used by another, more powerful than they. And who should the *real* villain be, of course, but my husband? "And what exactly was it that Dr Lopez was plotting?" my Lord Essex asked Signor Ferreira. "Oh, anything, anything at all," replied the good Ferreira, quick as a shot. "He has sworn to do anything King Philip might ask of him." Then Lord Essex, very cunning, asked, "Might he even poison the Queen, if the King of Spain asked it?" to which Signor Ferreira replied, "Of course." Then they asked Tinoco the same questions, with the rack before him, and he made the same replies. I had all this from Dr Nunez, who had it from Sir Robert Cecil himself.'

Robin and Philip stared at each other, each with the same thought in mind. Though Signor Ferreira's confession had been burned to ashes in their chimney-piece, that of Tinoco still existed, and was probably safe with Lord Essex. And a good man could be condemned on the evidence of *one* perjured rogue. Unless, of course, he had friends in high places, as Dr Lopez had . . .

'But the Cecils will protect Dr Lopez,' said Robin quickly. '*They* are his friends. *They* believe him innocent. You told me so yourself, Madam, only a short time ago.'

Mistress Lopez's eyes filled with tears. 'They *did* believe him innocent,' she replied, 'but now they have abandoned him. It was all too fantastical, too far-fetched, they said . . . the idea that my husband should be *pretending* for England's sake to be a spy for Spain, and this at Lord Walsingham's request. My Lord Walsingham, alas, is not alive to prove it. So the Cecils have gone over to Essex's side, even though they hate Lord Essex as much as Lord Essex hates them. They have a common enemy now.'

'But it is all lies!' Philip broke in. 'Dr Lopez will deny it, and the Queen . . . surely the Queen will believe him!'

Mistress Lopez was silent for a moment, but her cheeks grew hot and red, as if in shame.

'He admitted it,' she said at last.

The boys stared at her, aghast.

'*Admitted* it?' gulped Robin. 'Surely you can't mean that he . . . that he . . .'

Surprisingly, Mistress Lopez almost laughed. 'Of course I don't mean that he is guilty,' she said. 'Only that he admitted to being guilty, which is not quite the same thing.'

'But *why* . . . ?' Robin began, almost indignantly.

'It is easy for you to ask why . . . *you*, a strong lad with a head full of audacious dreams!' Mistress Lopez replied, and she sounded angry now. 'When you are old and frail, and used to living in peace and honour . . . when the years of conflict and danger are far behind you . . . then it is not so easy to be a hero. And when good friends turn to enemies and you are brought face to face with the rack and the torturer, then it is not easy at all.'

The boys looked at her in horror.

'The rack?' gasped Philip at last. 'They threatened Dr Lopez with the rack? How did they *dare*?'

Mistress Lopez sighed.

'They dare do anything – and to anyone,' she said. 'And if they will your death, then nothing can save you . . . not white hair, or royal blood, or even innocence itself. They showed my husband the rack, and he confessed to everything . . . everything . . . just to rid himself of the sight of it . . . and when he was safely back in his cell he retracted all that he had said. In any case, it doesn't matter. Nothing matters. Whether he pleads guilty or not guilty, the outcome will be the same.'

'How can it be the same, Madam?' asked Robin, puzzled.

'Because no one who is charged with High Treason is ever acquitted, except through a miracle.'

The words sounded strangely familiar. It occurred to Robin that he had once heard Dr Lopez say the very same thing. But what did it mean? Robin felt bewildered, and behind the bewilderment there lurked a dreadful fear. He now realized for the first time that the Doctor's life was in danger. The thought had sometimes come to him in the past, and he had quickly brushed it aside. But now he found himself thinking of the traitors' heads at the Southwark end of the Bridge, swinging to and fro on their poles at the mercy of every passing breeze.

When Robin found himself alone with Father, he asked the question that had been troubling him for so long.

101

'Mistress Lopez said that no one charged with High Treason was ever acquitted, except through a miracle,' he said. 'That can't be true, can it?'

Father looked grave.

'Her Majesty's ministers worry day and night about her safety,' he said at last, 'and they must do all in their power to protect her. That is why they would rather execute ten innocent men than allow one traitor to escape.'

'But that's not fair!' said Robin indignantly. 'What about the innocent man? What about his family? What about justice?'

Father smiled.

'When you are older,' he said, 'you will know better than to expect justice in this world. The Queen's ministers are not concerned with justice – they are only concerned with preserving her life. Do you know how many people have plotted and conspired against her since she came to the throne? Do you know how many times the assassin's knife has been turned away just in time? Let my Lord Burghley fail in his duties as a watchdog just *once*, and the Queen will die and this country will be plunged back into chaos. There were fearful wars of succession fought here only a hundred years ago – they called them the Wars of the Roses. People speak of them still, and shudder. Do you want those days to come again?'

'But we are not talking about some horrible assassin . . . we're talking about Dr Lopez. *Our* Dr Lopez. The Queen's physician. My friend.'

Father put his hand on Robin's shoulder.

'The Queen will find a new physician,' he said, 'and you will find a new friend. It is not *that* which worries me. No, I am more concerned about . . .'

'About what, Father?'

'About us, my son. About the secret Jews of St Olave's. I

have certain fears, and I can only pray that they will not be realized.'

'Are we in special danger, then? More danger than usual?'

Father sighed.

'Sit down,' he said at last. 'I want to talk to you. It is time, I think, that you knew more about our sufferings in the Old Country. I have kept silent long enough. You are not a child any more.'

The Fernandez children knew little about the great wave of persecution that had brought their parents to England, and their grandparents to the stake. Father and Mother liked to talk about the joys of their former life, the blue skies and orange groves of Portugal, and the Court officials, scholars and rich merchants who had been their friends there. But they changed the subject when the talk turned to harsher things, and Robin, Philip and Frances knew only that their parents had escaped and their grandparents died, and that the same fate threatened all those New Christians found guilty of returning secretly to Judaism. Now, as Father began for the first time to tell the full story of that dreadful era, Robin felt his blood run cold.

He heard about Jews baptized by force; about massacres; about Jews expelled from their homelands, and Jewish children sold into slavery. He heard how those Jews who became Christians were nicknamed 'Marranos' because it meant 'pigs' or 'accursed ones'. He heard how the Inquisition persuaded Christians to spy on their Marrano neighbours, and how those suspected of practising Judaism in secret were first tortured into confessing, and then burned at the stake in a great public spectacle known as the 'auto da fé'.

'All walls and windows had ears,' added Father, 'and the slightest suspicion of keeping the Jewish faith was enough. Clean clothes or an empty hearth on the Sabbath, for example . . . Our neighbours would watch chimneys for any sign of smoke. My own mother died because she was discovered putting a fresh tablecloth on the table one Friday night. A neighbour came in, and saw it. She was arrested, tortured, and burned in front of a crowd of sightseers. My father was burned because he refused to eat pork. Thousands of Marranos died that way – not all of them adults. Some of the victims of those acts of faith were children, younger than you, younger even than Philip.'

Robin sat looking at Father, unable to speak.

'I was a young man at that time – seventeen years old,' continued Father. 'My aunt and uncle took me to live with them, and we decided that the time had come to leave Portugal. We slipped away one night, and joined a crowd of other refugees on board a hired ship bound for England. Your mother was among them – *her* mother had been killed in a street riot and her father sold as a galley slave. We were at sea for three weeks, tossing on the waves, short of food and clean drinking water, seasick, dirty, and always in fear of being followed, captured, and taken back to Portugal. Some of the weaker passengers died during the journey. When we finally arrived in Bristol, where some of us had kinsfolk, even those who had survived were more dead than alive . . .'

'And did you like Bristol?' asked Robin.

'It was a fine city, and we were happy there. We are happy in England. But we can never forget Portugal. No one can ever forget his homeland.'

'But if we are happy in England, then why are we still afraid?'

'Because the practice of Judaism has been outlawed ever since King Edward I expelled the Jews from England in 1290. Besides, most of the people here still hate Jews. They think of us as monsters who drink Christian blood and poison wells.'

'But the Queen doesn't hate Jews, does she?' asked Robin anxiously. 'She used to trust Dr Lopez.'

Father smiled.

'Oh, the Queen is different,' he said. 'The Queen is wiser than other people. I think she would allow us to worship freely, if she could. But even *she* has to bow to the will of the people. Have I ever told you how she welcomed Maria Nunez, the beautiful Marrano?'

'No, I don't think so.'

'Maria and her brother were fleeing from the Inquisition in Spain, where their parents had been burned, and were on their way to Amsterdam, when their ship was seized by an English vessel and brought ashore. The Queen heard about Maria, and asked to see her. She was so charmed by Maria's beauty that she drove with her through the streets of London in the royal coach, and then invited her to stay in England. But Maria wanted to be able to practise Judaism openly, so she continued to Amsterdam, where she returned to her ancient faith. I remember now . . . I told Frances that story, not you . . . She loved it.'

Robin laughed.

'She would,' he said. 'But *I* love it too. Out of all the stories you have just told me, Father, I like that one the best.'

Father's fears *were* realized. Next day one of the windows in Master Mendes's house was shattered by a stone; the following day Dr Nunez found the word 'Jew' daubed on his front door. Everyone knew by now that Dr Lopez had been accused of plotting to poison the Queen; everyone was eager to condemn him. 'Lopez the Jew' they called him. 'Lopez the Jew,' they sang. Pamphlets showing dark faces with long, hooked noses sprouted on the bookstalls in Paul's Church-yard; ribald ballads about Jews were sung in the streets, and it was rumoured that Christopher Marlowe's play, *The Jew of Malta* was to be revived on the London stage.

'I saw it once in Bristol,' said Father, 'and it was a hideous experience. The Jew in the play was a monster, but the audience accepted it as truth, and they shouted and jeered.'

'But how do they know that Dr Lopez is a secret Jew?' asked Robin. 'He became a New Christian many years ago.'

'They don't know,' replied Father gravely, 'and if they did know it would be worse for all of us. But he was born a Jew, and that is enough for them in their present mood.'

'But you once said it was no crime to be born a Jew, so long as one embraced Christianity,' Robin persisted.

'I admit that . . . when times are normal. Times are not normal today. A former Jew stands accused of High Treason, and all these loyal citizens remember that he was born in a different country and a different faith. If he were black they would even now be singing rude songs about the Moors. If he were a Moslem they would be smashing the windows of the Arabian envoy. But he is a Jew, and so we Jews have become the target of their patriotism.'

'You don't think they would *kill* us?' asked Philip, feeling his knees trembling in spite of all his brave efforts to keep them steady.

'We shall be safe as long as we are careful. Speak as little as possible to your schoolmates . . . keep silent if you hear them talk about Lopez the Jew . . . never betray yourselves with a look or a word. And, Robin, it would be better if you gave up this theatrical nonsense for the time being.'

'Yes, Father,' said Robin, and for once he did not feel inclined to argue. London, his lovely London, had become an evil place, and Dr Lopez might not be the only victim of the Lopez conspiracy.

A few days later, special prayers were recited in the synagogue for the life of Dr Lopez and the safety of his fellow-Jews.

The synagogue in St Olave's was not really a synagogue at all. It bore no resemblance, Father said, to the ones left

106

behind in Spain and Portugal, now either destroyed or converted into Christian churches. Those synagogues had been magnificent houses of prayer, similar in style to the Moorish mosques with their slender columns and high engraved arches, their decorations of gold and silver filigree, and their sumptuous tiling representing fruit, flowers and trees – for, like Moslems, the Jewish artists were not allowed to depict human forms. The synagogue in St Olave's was only a room in the home of the Turkish diplomatic envoy Solomon Cormano, hidden away on an upper floor so that strangers could not easily find it. Here a curtained cupboard, representing the Ark of the Covenant, held the scrolls of the Law, which were encased in between silver and hung with tiny bells. Like the prayerbooks, these had been smuggled in by Marranos visiting London on their way to Holland or Belgium. Above the Ark a small lamp, known as the eternal light, burned continuously, and a Hebrew slogan spelt out the words, 'Know before whom thou standest.' A grille had been erected to separate the men from the women, according to custom. It was the men – very unfairly, thought Frances – who sat in the forefront of the room, close to the Ark, while the women had to content themselves with peering through the tiny gaps in the grille.

But on this occasion there were more momentous things to think about. When Master Pereira, a cloth merchant and a respected member of the community, arrived at the synagogue with his arm in bandages and scratches on his face, it became clear that the outbreak of anti-Jewish anger was already turning towards violence. A group of young men, taunting him with the words 'vile Jew', he explained, had set upon him in the street. Only the arrival of a good priest, who had pleaded with them to desist, had saved him from a worse beating.

'At least you were not killed,' said Master Cansino, a mild little man with a wispy white beard. 'My neighbour threatened me with death only last evening. For ten years we have been friends . . . he even invited me to his son's wedding. And he *knew* I was a New Christian. He has asked me many friendly questions about the old faith. Now he is so incensed against Jews that he waylaid me yesterday and threatened to cut my throat if any harm should befall the Queen. "Kill *me*?" I asked him. "Do you think *I* would injure the Queen? I am the same harmless old man that I always was!" "You Jewish pigs are all the same," he answered. "You killed Christ, and now you seek to kill our beloved Queen. You all deserve to die."'

'And what of my window?' broke in Master Mendes before anyone else could speak. 'The finest window in all Hart Street . . . it cost me twenty crowns. My wife is distraught. I never saw the villain who threw the stone, or else I should have thrashed him.' And Master Mendes puffed himself up till he looked like a turkey-cock, causing Robin and Philip to giggle despite all their fears.

But soon the solemnity of the gathering engulfed them again. The men, wrapped in white silk prayer shawls, huddled over their prayerbooks, which were written partly in Hebrew, partly in a Latin dialect called Ladino. As the old cantor, Master Alvaro, lifted his quavering voice in prayers of intercession for the life of Rodrigo Lopez, a wailing cry arose from the women in the darkness behind the grille. 'O deliver us from every enemy, ambush and hurt by the way, and from all afflictions that visit and trouble the world,' chanted the worshippers. 'Behold, He that guardeth Israel shall neither slumber nor sleep.'

Dr Lopez was brought to trial on a clear, frosty day in February, and the Marrano community of London held its breath, and prayed, and waited. In the streets the excited populace sang songs, jeered, ate hot pies, and shouted, 'Down with the Jew!' Everyone knew what the outcome of

108

the trial would be, but the waiting itself was almost as good as an execution.

The one thing that consoled Mistress Lopez in all her misery was the knowledge that Signor Ferreira and Tinoco had also been charged with High Treason and were to stand trial with her husband. 'The perjured rogues hoped to save their own lives by denouncing him,' she told Robin and Philip, 'but they have gained nothing, except shame and contempt.'

The trial, which took place in Essex House, was held in secret, but Dr Nunez was allowed to be there, and it was he who brought the verdict to the homes – one by one – of all the Marrano families of London. By the time he reached the Fernandez household he was tired and frozen almost to the bone, and he was grateful to draw up his chair to the hearth and accept a steaming cup of mulled wine.

'The news I bring you is no more than we expected, Master Fernandez,' he said at last.

'Then Dr Lopez is condemned,' replied Father, and the two boys felt their blood run cold.

'How could it be otherwise?' asked Dr Nunez sadly. 'He was allowed no lawyers . . . no counsel . . . nothing, and all those brilliant, probing minds – the Cecils, Francis and Anthony Bacon, and my Lord Essex himself – were ranged against him. The greatest legal minds in England all set to entrap one helpless old man. Indeed, never have I seen him look so old.'

'And what was the evidence?' asked Father, trying to sound calm.

'Very little, apart from his own confession – which he had in any case retracted – and identical confessions signed by those two scoundrels who were tried with him.'

'*Two* confessions?' cried Robin. 'But there couldn't have been two. We burned one of them . . .' And then he clapped his hand to his mouth, fearful that he might have said too much.

'It is just as well that Dr Nunez is a friend,' said Father drily, 'or you might have got us hanged. But as you have said so much already, Dr Nunez may as well know the rest.'

'A fine adventure indeed,' said their visitor approvingly, after Father had told him the full story of Philip's escapade. 'But there were *two* confessions, and both were read aloud in Court.'

'Then the one signed by Signor Ferreira is a forgery,' shouted Philip. 'When Lord Essex found that it was missing he must have got Master Forsham to write a new one.'

'We must go and tell my Lord Burghley at once,' cried Robin, his eyes gleaming. 'We must let him know that part of the evidence was forged . . .'

'You silly lad,' interrupted Dr Nunez, 'do you really think my Lord Burghley didn't know the evidence was forged? They *all* knew. It was *all* forged, or false, or obtained through torture. You don't imagine for one moment that this was intended to be a fair trial, do you?'

'But *why*? What do they have against him?'

'That is something we shall never know,' replied Dr Nunez with a sigh. 'But we can do nothing to help him – we must think of ourselves now. I am afraid there may be trouble. Dunstan Ames is planning to leave the country – he says he can no longer afford the luxury of being known as Rodrigo Lopez's father-in-law. And several others will follow him – Antonio Costa Olivario, I think, and also Pinto de Britto. They are frightened, and I cannot blame them. Already the people are shouting 'Jews!' in the streets.'

'Yes, we have heard them,' said Father. 'But what of Mistress Lopez? What will she do now?'

'Ah, she is a true wife. Master Ames tried to persuade her to leave England with him, but she refuses to go. She says that as long as her husband is alive her place is in the same city, and under the same sky.'

The words 'as long as her husband is alive' made Robin shiver. There was one question he had to ask, and yet he did not want to know the answer.

'Sir, what is going to happen to Dr Lopez?' he asked at last, forcing himself to say the words.

'He has been found guilty of High Treason, he and those two other unfortunates,' replied Dr Nunez, 'and for High Treason there is only one possible sentence.'

Although he expected this reply, Robin felt as if he were going to faint. He knew well enough what the sentence was for High Treason. Condemned traitors were dragged on a hurdle to the gallows at Tyburn, and there hanged, drawn and quartered. It did not bear thinking about for any man, let alone his kind old friend.

Philip, being younger than Robin, forgot his recent heroic deeds and began to cry.

'Have courage, my young gallant,' said Dr Nunez, patting his head. 'There is still one hope left.' Then, as both boys looked at him eagerly, he went on, 'I mean Her Majesty. No one can touch Dr Lopez until she signs his death-warrant. And how if she were to refuse to sign? How if she were to remember that she was once his good friend?'

Chapter Nine

The Queen did not sign the death-warrant, and Dr Lopez went on living for the time being. Winter gave way to Spring; the ice melted from the Thames, and pink and white blossom formed again in the orchards that bordered the river. May Day came with its hobby-horses and maypoles and Morris dancers; every house was wreathed in flowers and green branches, and schoolboys and apprentices, enjoying an unaccustomed day of release from the daily grind, sang, 'O month of May, the merry month of May' as they tumbled and jostled each other in the sunlit streets.

So it was not surprising that the Fernandez children should think less and less about Dr Lopez as the weeks passed. Their elders still wore grave faces and conversed in whispers . . . but then, old people were always like that, solemn and secretive in their furred robes and stiff farthingales. It must be awful, thought Robin, to be old.

Soon after May Day, something happened that almost put the Lopez troubles right out of the boys' heads. They were invited to take part as choristers in a masque to be held at Whitehall Palace in the presence of the Queen herself. The great Gloriana would be both their hostess and the chief member of their audience, and the thought of it made them tremble.

At first they were afraid that Father might not allow them to go. Had he not insisted that Robin must give up his 'theatrical nonsense' until times were normal again? But, much to the boys' surprise, he was delighted by the invitation.

'Nothing like this has ever happened in our family before,' he said, stroking his beard with satisfaction. 'Our ancestors, of course, knew many honours – one of my great-uncles was physician to the Duke of Castile, and my great-great-grandfather was stabbed to death by a prince of Estoril during a civic brawl – but to be commanded to attend on the sovereign . . . no, no, I must admit that we have never known *quite* so high an honour till now. I wonder what Master Mendes will say. None of his offspring can sing a note. Indeed, Thomas, poor lad, can hardly talk either.'

'You must have new cloaks and doublets,' broke in Mother eagerly. 'I shall go to Cheapside this very day to buy the most expensive velvet they have. Or might one of the shops in the Bridge have a better selection? I can't have Her Majesty receiving you at Whitehall in anything but the best velvet.'

Robin, laughing, explained that the choristers would probably have to wear identical livery chosen by the Master of the Revels, and Mother's face dropped in disappointment.

'The *same* as all those others? Not even an ounce more of braid or embroidery on your cloak, and Philip's? Then how can the Queen pick you out for special attention, if you all look alike?'

'In these times,' remarked Father drily, 'it may be better if the Queen does *not* single anyone out for special attention. We know well enough that special attention can lead to the block or the gallows.'

But Mother was too excited to listen to anything Father had to say. 'You will have to stretch up tall and sing your loudest and best,' she told the boys, 'and then perhaps Her Majesty will notice you and ask for you to come and sing to her again. After that . . . who knows? Courtiers have risen from humbler beginnings than ours.'

There was one person in the Fernandez household who did not join in the general excitement, and that was Frances. Her marriage to Thomas Mendes had been fixed for the end of July, and it seemed to her that Time was racing faster and faster to meet the day she so much dreaded. She and Thomas had seen each other several times since their betrothal, but had not come to know or like each other any better. Thomas still quoted Latin each time they met, bowing stiffly as he handed her some gift his mother had chosen. 'But we've never *spoken* to each other, never had a real conversation,' Frances complained to her mother, 'so how can I marry him, be mistress at his table and the mother of his children, and live with him for the rest of my life?'

'Thousands of women do it,' replied Mother calmly, 'so why not you? And you will have a fine house and many servants, jewels and farthingales, and bear an honoured name. Don't take it so much to heart, child. *I* did not love your father when I married him, but now I am as merry as the day is long. Indeed, I am too busy to be anything else.'

That, at least, seemed true enough. As the wedding day approached, Mother spent more and more time giving orders to the servants as they stitched away at the trousseau and bridal garments, made sweetmeats and preserves, and prepared the house for the marriage feast. But longer than the hours she spent with the servants were those she devoted to

114

Frances, teaching her the many accomplishments a housewife needed to know.

She had, in the first place, to be in full command of the kitchen, the dairy and distillery. The servants did the ordinary, everyday cooking, but the mistress of the house always made her own pickles and preserves, jams and marmalades, jellies and cordials. She had to know how to make syrups out of rose and violet petals, and candied flowers and comfits; gingerbreads and almond butter and delicate puff pastry, and marchpane beautifully gilded and decorated.

A housewife also had to make her own soap, using rose-leaves and lavender-flowers and scenting it with oil of almonds or musk, as well as toothpaste and mouth-washes, which were usually concocted from such ingredients as honey, vinegar and white wine boiled together. (The heads of mice, burned to ashes, were also said to make an excellent powder for cleaning the teeth, but for some reason Mother never tried this particular recipe.)

Perhaps most important of all, the mistress of the house had to be skilled in making medicines and ointments, for it was her duty to look after the health of everyone in the household. Frances found this part of her education a sad task, for she could not help thinking of poor Dr Lopez as she gathered herbs in the kitchen-garden or mixed sherry sack with salad oil and boiled snails to make a cure for the gout.

As well as being cook, confectioner and apothecary, a lady also had to be clever at her needlework. During these last few crowded months before her wedding, Frances stitched away at tapestries and learned how to embroider cushions with gold and silver thread and make elaborate 'cut work' lace, most of which went into ruffs and cuffs and collars for her trousseau.

Thinking of Thomas Mendes, with his solemn white face and black doublet and Latin orations, Frances took little pleasure in learning how to be a good wife to him. But the invitation that came to Robin and Philip from Whitehall Palace was the most crushing blow of all. It seemed to her that life offered everything that was lovely and new and exciting to her brothers, and everything that was drab and dull and burdensome to herself.

Frances's feelings of being ill-used grew stronger as the weeks passed and the boys kept coming home from rehearsals for the Royal masque full of excited descriptions of the marvels that awaited them at Whitehall.

Masques usually had elaborate settings, and those intended for the Queen's pleasure were the most elaborate of all. 'We have a real castle in one scene – made of canvas, of course, but so painted that you would think it were solid stone,' said Robin, excitedly, as the family sat at supper on the day of the first dress rehearsal. 'And we have a galleon in another scene, with great, billowing sails and golden oars and a blue painted ocean to sail on . . .'

'And a street of houses, canvas houses, with open windows and candles shining through,' added Philip eagerly.

'And we have *three* changes of costume – red velvet and white satin; turquoise satin embroidered with gold, and a scene where we play gods and goddesses in sea-green draperies . . .' Robin began, only to be interrupted by shrieks of laughter from the family.

'And which do you two play – the gods or the goddesses?' asked Father as soon as he could speak. 'No, don't tell me . . . I'll wager you'll be wenches again, flouncing about in skirts. You always are, for some reason that I can't fathom.'

'That's because they have pretty faces,' said Frances, and in the scuffle that followed she found herself feeling quite young and cheerful again.

But her elation did not last long. Next day, Father and Mother received an invitation to a family wedding in Bristol; it meant that they would be away from home for about three weeks, and that they would miss seeing the boys set out for Whitehall.

'My sons are to be received by the Queen for the first time in their lives,' lamented Mother, 'and *I*, poor creature, cannot have the privilege of seeing them on their way. Never mind . . . Jennet will see to it that your necks are clean and your hair properly brushed, and you can be sure that our thoughts and prayers will go with you all the way from Bristol. As for you, Frances, I'll not worry about you being idle while I am away, for you have plenty to do. Sarah has promised to teach you how to make quince marmalade and chilblain ointment, and you have that tapestry to finish and three dozen chemises to hem.'

So that is our lives arranged for us – for Father and Mother, an exciting journey and a wedding; for Robin and Philip, music and feasting in a Royal palace, and for me, chilblain ointment and three dozen chemises to hem, thought Frances, blinking away tears of anger and frustration. Oh, it isn't fair . . . it isn't fair. It's not much that I ask, after all . . . If I could have just *one* exciting thing happen to me, *one* adventure, *one* lovely day that I could always remember, I could even reconcile myself to marrying that dreary Thomas. Just *one* little adventure to look back on – but where is it to come from?

Father and Mother set out for Bristol on a sunny morning in early June, their coach laden with splendid gifts; almost the entire contents of their wardrobe; goblets and plates and eating utensils; and what seemed like half the food and drink in the house. They would be spending their nights at inns along the way, and when travelling they always tried to observe the dietary laws of the Jewish religion by taking their own meals with them. The body of the coach sank lower and lower into the wheels as each fresh load and package was placed aboard, and Mother looked at the whole contraption

117

anxiously and said that she hoped the horses would be strong enough to pull it.

'I asked for them to be given a double portion of oats this morning,' Father replied with a twinkle, 'so the good beasts might be as strong as Hercules.'

'I know we are going to be jolted most horribly,' Mother went on, not at all mollified. 'I hate travelling by coach.'

'Until we learn to fly, this is the only way we have of making long journeys,' replied Father. 'We can only pray that there will be no more weddings in our family for many years to come – always excepting our Frances's wedding, which of course gives us such joy.' Here Father smiled kindly at Frances, who found it hard to smile back.

The wedding to which he and Mother were travelling would actually be *two* weddings, for New Christians who practised Judaism in secret had to lead a double life. The bride and bridegroom would plight their troth openly in a church, in the presence of all their friends and neighbours, with Christian prayers and anthems and Christian clergy to join their hands. But first they would hurry to the hidden synagogue in a Marrano house, where a Rabbi would be waiting to perform a Jewish ceremony and present them with a marriage contract written in ancient Aramaic. Here, the bridegroom would place the ring on his bride's hand – this time on a different finger – and then take her for his wife 'according to the law of Moses and of Israel', as they stood together under a specially erected bridal canopy.

But even ordinary weekends brought their share of double religious observance, the synagogue services on Saturdays being followed by church on Sundays with a sermon for schoolboys to memorize in preparation for school on those terrifying Monday mornings.

It was this, Robin often thought, that made life especially hard for him and Philip. They had to learn about both religions, being thrashed by the Rabbi when they made mistakes in their Hebrew, and by Master Breakstaff when they did not know their Catechism or forgot some point in the sermon. It was difficult to know who had the stronger right arm or the sharper tongue, Master Breakstaff or the Rabbi. And it had been little comfort to learn from Dr Lopez that Hebrew was now a fashionable language at Court, and that the Queen herself was an accomplished Hebrew scholar. No one, thought Robin, ever dared thrash the Queen for not knowing her Hebrew grammar.

Before Father and Mother left, the whole family joined them in prayers for a safe journey. Travelling was a dangerous as well as a tiring business; ruts and mire and badly-made roads were not the only perils that awaited those who were foolhardy enough to venture beyond the walls of the city. There were robbers and footpads lurking in the belts of the forest that edged the highway, and ragged and hideous vagrants and beggars of all kinds, from the Counterfeit Cranks and Palliards, who painted sores and wounds on their limbs and swathed themselves in filthy bandages, to the Abraham-Men who pretended to be mad and roamed the countryside half-naked and howling. Then there were the tinkers and pedlars, picking their customers' pockets under the guise of selling them little trinkets; and the bear-wards, almost as fierce as the beasts they led on chains, and jugglers and fortune-tellers and minstrels singing the kind of cheeky ballad on the village green that they would not dare sing in any stately dining-chamber. And so, even though their coach-driver carried a stout cudgel, Mother and Father felt that a prayer or two would not come amiss before they went on their way.

On the morning of the Royal masque, Frances was woken by an urgent knocking at her door.

Her visitor was Robin, still in his nightgown, and looking pale and distraught.

119

'It's Philip,' he gasped as soon as she opened the door. 'He's ill . . . he says he has a terrible stomach-ache, and he keeps being sick. Oh, what shall we do . . . why isn't Mother here?'

'Don't be such a child,' said Frances with dignity. For some reason that she could not explain, she felt completely calm. 'I'm nearly a married woman, and I know all about medicines. Mother taught me.'

'But you've never cured anyone yet.'

'I've never killed anyone either, and not many physicians can say as much.'

Robin looked at Frances hopefully.

'Can you come and see him, then?' he asked. 'Sarah is with him already, and *she* thinks he has the Evil Eye.'

Sarah, the housekeeper, was weeping and wringing her hands at Philip's bedside as Frances and Robin entered. Philip was lying back among the lavender-scented pillows, his eyes closed, and his face a delicate shade of green.

'I knew this was going to happen,' wailed Sarah as soon as she saw the children. 'It's that Mistress Mendes . . . who else? *Her* two whey-faced sons were not chosen to sing for our Lady the Queen, and so she grew jealous and took her revenge on our poor Philip. Look at him . . . I'll wager she's made a wax image of him and is sticking pins in it. That's why he keeps getting pains in his stomach, poor lamb.'

'Sarah, you mustn't talk like that about my future mother-in-law,' said Frances, putting on her most grown-up voice. 'Mistress Mendes is a gracious lady, and I won't have you calling her a witch.'

'But . . .'

'It's more likely that he's over-excited at the idea of appearing before the Queen. Too much excitement always makes Philip sick.'

'No . . . no . . . it's not excitement . . . it was the plums,' mumbled Philip, lifting his head from the pillows and then letting it fall back again as another wave of sickness surged over him.

'Plums? What plums?' asked Frances, surprised. 'The plums in the orchard aren't ripe yet.'

'I know. That's why they made me ill.'

'Have you been raiding the orchard, you jackanapes?' shouted Sarah, forgetting all her sympathy and advancing on the sickbed menacingly.

Philip began to cry.

'I only had a few,' he sobbed. 'About ten, or maybe twelve, that's all.'

'*Twelve?*'

'Well, they *looked* ripe, and I'd eaten them all before I realized that they weren't.'

Robin began to laugh, but caught Sarah's eye and coughed instead.

'Well, it's a good dose of my special stomach cordial for you, my lad,' said Sarah sternly, and Philip groaned again, though not from pain this time. All the children hated Sarah's special stomach cordial. It contained boiled spiders, fishbones and the blood of a white hen, and it tasted awful.

When Sarah had left to fetch the cordial, Robin looked at Philip and sighed.

'I suppose you know this means you won't be able to go to the Palace?' he said.

'I might feel better after I've had Sarah's cordial.'

'You'll probably feel worse. Anyway, we can't take the risk. Suppose you were sick all over the Queen's floor . . . She might have your head cut off. And mine too.'

Philip started to cry again.

'But I *can't* miss going to the Palace,' he wailed. 'I might never get the chance again.'

'You should have thought of that before you stole the plums.'

'But . . .'

121

'He *shall* go.'

It was Frances who spoke, and the two boys looked at her in amazement. Her voice sounded quite strange, and there was an odd light in her eyes.

'But Frances, how can he?' said Robin. 'He's too ill even to get out of bed.'

'I know that. He'll go, but it won't be him.'

'What are you talking about?'

'It will be me.'

'*You*? But how . . .?'

'It came to me just now, like a flash of lightning. Don't you see, Robin? This is my big chance . . . to have an adventure, just *one*, before I settle down to married life with that boring Thomas. You wouldn't grudge me that, would you?'

'But I still don't understand . . .'

'Boys dress up as girls in your theatre, so why shouldn't a girl dress up as a boy for a change? I'm the same size as Philip, and we look alike . . . everyone says so.'

Robin stared at Frances, and realized that it was true. Philip was tall for his age, and Frances was small for hers. They both had the same hazel eyes and the same mop of short, crisp brown curls. They could be twins. They could almost be the same person.

'When Philip wears a woman's dress he looks exactly like me,' Frances went on eagerly. 'So if I were to wear a doublet, why shouldn't I look exactly like him?'

'No, no, it's a crazy idea,' replied Robin. 'You haven't been to any of the rehearsals . . . you wouldn't know what to do.'

'I'll just watch the others, and do as they do.'

'You don't know the songs.'

'Yes I do – I've heard you two sing them often enough.'

'And how would you explain your absence to the servants?'

122

'That's easy. I'll tell Sarah that Mistress Lopez has invited me to spend the day with her. She won't object to that.'

'No, but she might object to seeing you leave home dressed as a boy!'

'She won't see me. I've thought of that. I shall leave home in my own clothes, go to the corner of the street, then creep back and wait outside the door. As soon as Sarah is busy in the dairy, you shall let me back into the house. I shall change into Philip's clothes, leave the house and then wait at the corner again while you say good-bye to Sarah and the servants. It's all quite simple, really.'

'It doesn't *sound* simple . . .' Robin began, and then broke off as Sarah came back into the bedchamber, carrying a pewter tankard containing an evil-looking reddish brew. Philip yelled and dived under the bedclothes, and Frances and Robin had to hold him still while Sarah poured her special cordial down his unwilling throat.

As soon as breakfast had been eaten, Frances told Sarah that she was going to spend the day with Mistress Lopez.

'I'm glad of that,' replied Sarah, 'for she has little enough to comfort her, poor lady. Take her some of the almond comfits you made yesterday, and tell her we are all praying that the good doctor may soon be pardoned.' And Sarah smiled so approvingly that Frances felt almost ashamed to be deceiving her.

But I *deserve* an adventure, she told herself firmly as she waited outside the house for Robin to let her back in. It seemed ages before the door opened a few inches and his face peered out anxiously.

'Sarah *would* keep talking instead of attending to her chores . . . she says she's going to give Philip a good whipping as soon as he's better,' Robin explained as he and Frances crept upstairs to his bedchamber. Philip was asleep, but his best clothes were spread out on the lid of his chest. Robin watched in trepidation as Frances struggled into them. He had to help her tie the points of her doublet and hose and fasten the cord that attached her cloak to her left shoulder, but on the whole – he hated to admit it – she managed the transformation quite well.

'And you really do look like Philip!' he added. 'It's quite amazing. Now, are you sure you'll be able to tie your own points next time? Remember, we shall have three changes of costume, and I shan't be able to help you with the other boys watching.'

Frances nodded happily. She was sure everything was going to proceed according to plan. It was strange that Robin, the courageous firstborn son, should be so much more nervous than she was. Waiting for him at the corner of Hart Street, she was glad to observe that not a single passerby threw her so much as a glance. 'My disguise must be a good one,' she thought, throwing back her shoulders so that her cloak flared in the breeze, and admiring her legs in their sleek silk hose. It was not long before Robin joined her, looking flustered and out of breath.

'All the servants had to see me on my way,' he said, 'and Jennet cried so much – with happiness, she said – that she swallowed one of her teeth. And Sarah wanted to hang a dead bat around my neck to ward off the Evil Eye, but I wouldn't let her . . .'

'A dead bat?' giggled Frances. 'Where did she find it?'

'I don't know, but she insisted that she had been saving it especially for today.'

'Poor Sarah. It was cruel of you to disappoint her.'

'Poor Sarah indeed,' said Robin crossly. 'It's *me* you should be pitying. I had been looking forward to this masque, and now I shall be trembling all the time in case you are discovered. Suppose any of the boys should realize that you are not Philip – what then?'

'You don't suppose they would betray me, do you?'

124

replied Frances, laughing. 'Why, anyone who has any love of adventure will support me in this last bid for freedom.'

'But adventures are for boys, for men and boys,' said Robin. 'I love adventure as much as any other lad, but not for girls . . . girls belong in the house, doing their cooking and embroidery.'

'You should tell that to our Lady the Queen,' replied Frances, stepping nimbly out of the way to avoid a basinful of slops that someone had just thrown from an upper window. She felt so unusually light on her feet that she wished she need never wear a heavy skirt and petticoats again.

All the choristers were to meet at Blackfriars, where a splendid boat with gilded oars and a scarlet-striped awning was waiting to take them to Whitehall. 'Now, remember not to talk too much,' hissed Robin in Frances's ear as they stepped aboard. 'Philip is a quiet sort of person – he never talks unless he has something important to say. And *do* sit with your knees apart, not clamped together in that mincing ladylike fashion.'

Robin's anxiety grew as the boat left Blackfriars and began to nose its way past Bridewell Palace and the glowing gardens of the Temple. One or two boys had glanced strangely at Frances and were now nudging each other and whispering, and he felt it might be as well to confide in them. Soon all the choristers on board knew Frances's secret, and – as Frances had expected – they were all hugely delighted.

'They are good lads, and won't give you away,' murmured Robin. 'It's more than you deserve, really.'

Frances smiled to herself, but did not answer. The boat had just passed Essex House, the scene of Philip's great adventure, and suddenly the idea came to her that something more than a mere escapade might be awaiting her at White-hall. Perhaps . . . perhaps she might even be allowed to do something to help Dr Lopez, waiting so patiently for death or pardon. Her heart lifted as the river curved and she saw the towers and spires of the Queen's palace advancing towards her across the shining water.

Chapter Ten

The Royal Palace of Whitehall was nearly as big as the city of London, outside whose walls it stood. On one side it was bounded by lush orchards and gardens and a long stretch of the river; on another side by the vast green acres of St James's park, the monarch's private hunting-grounds, and on a third side by the Palace of Westminster. The road that led from London to Westminster ran through the middle of the Palace grounds, surmounted at either side by a splendid archway.

The scarlet-canopied boat landed the choristers at the Garden Stairs, and from there the excited boys (and girl) stepped for the first time on to Royal territory. 'But it's not just a palace – it's a whole kingdom,' whispered Frances to Robin as an usher led them through what seemed like endless meadows and pastures. There were even houses in the grounds; and magnificent gates and towers and a chapel; and fountains and fishponds and dove-cotes, and tennis-courts, bowling alleys and a cockpit, and a tilt-yard overlooked by a tapestried gallery where the Queen and her courtiers, so the usher explained, sat to watch tournaments. And everywhere they saw royal attendants, pages and ushers, maids of honour in richly-embroidered wheel farthingales and servants in livery, moving with slow dignity amid the greenery of the Queen's garden like peacocks with their tails outspread or galleons in full sail.

But the grounds of Whitehall Palace were nothing compared with its interior. Nothing Robin had ever seen – not even Essex House, nothing Frances had ever dreamed of, could possibly have prepared them for the sight that greeted them after the usher had led them from the tiring-chamber, where they had changed into their costumes and refreshed themselves with ale and saffron cakes, into the great banqueting-hall where the masque was to take place.

Their first impression was that the hall was made entirely of gold. It flashed at them from the gold tracery on the ceiling, from the gold-embroidered tapestries and hangings on the walls, from the gold-threaded cushions and canopy on the Queen's still-empty chair. The light of hundreds of candles in gilded sconces and gold candlesticks shone on gold and silver plate; on chests and cabinets and ornaments of inlaid wood, coral and mother-of-pearl, crystal and ebony, ivory and exquisitely-painted enamel, and on the rich silks and brocades and jewels of the assembled courtiers. Yet the children were surprised to see that the floor of the hall – apart from a narrow red carpet leading from the door to the foot of the Queen's chair – was strewn with ordinary hay.

A great silence now lay over the company; nothing moved apart from the flicker of firelight and candlelight. It was as if the hundreds of people in the hall were woven into a living tapestry. She will be here in a moment, thought Frances. I have been waiting all my life for this day.

Suddenly a herald in scarlet livery approached the Royal

chair, and lifted a gold trumpet to his lips, and the sound of a fanfare pierced the silence like a sword.

A vision appeared in the doorway. Frances, her head bent as she bowed, imagined rather than saw it at first. Then she looked up in time to see the Queen move slowly into the hall, her twenty-four maids of honour gliding like swans behind her.

They were young and beautiful and dressed in white, but Frances – though she envied them with all her heart – had eyes only for the Queen. But she *is* Gloriana, she said to herself, almost in surprise, Gloriana, Queen of Fairyland, as all the poets call her.

The Queen, though no longer young, was as upright and stately as a goddess. She wore a marvellous gown of white satin embroidered with gold, and there were pearls round her neck and in her ears and a bird of paradise, studded with jewels, sat on her high-piled red hair. Her hands were beautiful – slim and white, and glittering with rings. But nothing compared with her smile. As she looked down at the assembly from her Royal chair, the radiance of her smile lit the hall so that all the candles and torches seemed superfluous.

It was because of the Queen's smile that Frances had her great idea.

It came to her half-way through the masque . . . just as the ocean scene was about to begin. One of the mermaids, a plump little boy in a pearl-embroidered tail that was a little too tight for him, became excited by the splendour of the occasion, leaped forward too quickly, tripped over his trailing fins, and fell flat on his face at the Queen's feet. The other mermaids gasped in horror, one of the dolphins laughed, and the little boy – aware that the Master of the Revels was scowling and shaking his fist at him from the back of the hall – began to cry.

129

But the Queen saved the situation. She stood up, stepped down from her gold-canopied chair, and helped the blushing mermaid to his feet, removing a wisp of hay from his hair as she did so, and smiling kindly.

'I wish all my subjects were so quick to serve me,' she said. 'Mistress Mermaid, I trust Poseidon will reward you for your zeal.' Her voice was just like her smile, rich and warm.

It was then that Frances knew what she had to do to save Dr Lopez. His life depended on the Queen's pardon, and the Queen had not yet signed his death warrant. Well then, she, Frances Fernandez, would seek out the Queen after the masque, and plead for him. It was plain that the great Queen was a kind and gentle lady, and she would not be angry. Besides, had she not once driven a golden coach through the streets of London with a beautiful Marrano Lady at her side?

'You're not singing . . . you haven't forgotten the words, have you?' an anxious voice hissed in her ear, and Frances turned to see Robin staring at her in dismay. She smiled back at him reassuringly, and began to sing as lustily as she could, but her thoughts were no longer on the masque, even though it was the most splendid entertainment she had ever seen.

Scene followed scene and song followed song; castles and galleons and gardens rose up and then vanished again under the gilded ceiling. Some of the courtiers began to look tired; one or two even yawned and hastily clapped their hands over their mouths, but the Queen never yawned once, and never stopped smiling. She applauded the torchlight procession, roared with laughter at the clowns, and graciously accepted a gold crown inscribed with the words, 'For the fairest' from a group of shivering choristers dressed as Grecian goddesses. And when the Master of the Revels finally closed the masque by reciting a long boring set of Latin verses, the Queen actually shook his hand and said, 'You must have had a good teacher, Master Sutcliffe . . . your Latin is better than mine.'

Yes, Elizabeth was all that her grateful subjects had ever said about her, and more. So why, now that the masque was over, should Frances begin to feel a sinking sensation in her stomach? It was not because she was hungry. A feast had been provided for the players and choristers, but as soon as she looked at the long table laden with roast meats and fishes, jellies, tarts and pies, she suddenly wanted to be sick.

No . . . she had to face the truth. Soon she would have to throw herself at the Royal feet and plead for Dr Lopez's life, and even though the Queen was a kind and gentle lady who smiled most graciously, Frances could not help feeling afraid.

When the masque and the feasting was over, the company danced in the long gallery. The Queen herself led the dancing, first with Lord Essex, and then with Sir Christopher Hatton and Sir Walter Raleigh, and although her partners grew tired, she never seemed to falter. The children were amazed to see how high she leaped in the lavolta, her face alight with enjoyment. 'It's almost as if she were flying,' Frances whispered to Robin. 'She's like a bird . . . or a goddess, surely.' To herself she added, But if she goes on dancing all day, how am I to reach her? I can't very well fall at her feet in front of all these courtiers and ladies. Oh please, God, make her tired . . . make her leave the gallery just for a few minutes, so I can follow her.

At last her prayer was answered. The Queen left, followed by her maids of honour, and the music and merriment suddenly stopped as all the company sank into deep bows and curtseys. As soon as she had gone the dancing began again, but it was as if a great light had gone out of the place, now that only the candles and torches were left to illuminate it.

'Where has she gone, do you think?' Frances asked Robin, suddenly aware that her idol had vanished into thin air.

'How should I know? Maybe to her bedchamber, to rest.

Maybe to her study, to read. Maybe to one of the State apartments, to receive an Ambassador or a delegation. Queens lead busy lives, you know.'

'Yes, I should have thought of that,' murmured Frances. 'We probably shan't see her again.' She should have felt sorry, and yet for some reason she was relieved. It was almost with a sense of disappointment that she saw Richard Lucy's face peer over Robin's shoulder and heard his pert voice say, '*I* know where the Queen is. You should have asked *me*, young fellow, instead of picking the brains of that stupid brother of yours.'

'Well, where *has* she gone, then?' asked Robin, a little nettled.

'The Queen walks in the garden every afternoon with one of her maids of honour. Except when it's raining, of course . . . and it isn't raining today.'

'Just one of her maids of honour? Doesn't she have soldiers to guard her?'

'Not when she goes walking. My father says she takes unnecessary risks, but the Queen insists that she must be freely available to her people. So if either of you were thinking of asking a favour, now is the time to seek her out.' And Richard turned away again, laughing uproariously at his joke.

Frances shivered. It was as if Richard were reading her mind. But how am I to go in search of the Queen? she asked herself. I can't pretend to be ill, Philip tried that trick already, at Essex House. I could say I need some fresh air. It's so hot in here . . . they must have lit at least a thousand candles. But suppose Robin should be afraid to let me out of his sight?

In the end, escape proved easier than she had expected. Robin did not try to stop her; probably, she thought ruefully, he was glad to be rid of her. No attendants stood in her way as she ran down the broad staircase that led to the vestibule and the world outside. No one even glanced at her as she wandered along the gravel paths of the knot garden, stopping at intervals to admire flower-beds ablaze with marigolds, carnations and gillyflowers, or to marvel at the intricate shapes and patterns into which the hedges had been carved.

But there was no time for her to relax and enjoy the garden. At any moment now she might come face to face with the Queen, and what was she to say in that almighty presence? 'May it please Your Majesty, I crave a boon . . .' No doubt every petitioner started like that, and she wanted to be different. She would be brave, and come directly to the point. 'Your Majesty, please spare Dr Lopez . . .' Yes, the Queen would like that. She had suffered dangers and hardships herself; she was a brave woman. And she would admire courage in others.

Frances suddenly quailed, aware that a large, fierce-looking lady in gold satin was bearing down on her. 'Boy, come here,' she called in a loud, shrill voice, and Frances approached reluctantly, wishing she had a skirt to hide the trembling of her knees.

'I don't know your face, boy,' snapped the lady, her gimlet eyes staring curiously at Frances. 'Whose page are you?'

'Er . . . Sir Christopher Hatton's, madam,' stammered Frances, grasping at the first name that came into her mind.

'Really? I thought the Fairfax boy was his page.'

'He . . . he's not very well today, and I'm taking his place.'

'Well, he's always been a sickly creature. They say a witch put a spell on him in his cradle. Tell me, when does the Queen move to Nonsuch Palace?'

'I . . . I'm afraid I don't know, madam,' said Frances, desperately looking round for some means of escape.

'You call yourself a courtier, and you *don't know*?' shrilled the lady indignantly. 'I'm beginning to despair of the young people of today . . . all you care about is football, and dressing up in gewgaws, and stuffing yourselves with sweetmeats. My grandson would make a better page than you, and I shall tell Sir Christopher so. Very well, be off with you.'

'Y-yes, madam,' gulped Frances, so relieved to be free of this she-dragon that she forgot which way she was going and ran back along the path she had just taken.

It was a fortunate mistake. At the end of the path was an arch entwined with roses, and even as she looked she saw a figure pass under the arch and move slowly towards her. It was a glittering figure, tall and stately as a goddess, with gold embroidery on its white satin gown and a jewelled bird of paradise on its high-piled red hair.

Frances's first reaction was to hide. She leaped behind a section of hedge cunningly trimmed in the shape of a lion rampant and crouched down on the grass, her heart thumping so violently that she felt sure the Queen could hear it.

After a few moments she felt brave enough to peer through a gap in the hedge, but saw nothing, apart from the golden glow of marigolds and the emerald sheen of the close-cropped lawn. Yet in a few minutes, she knew, the Queen would pass within a few inches of her, and she shut her eyes, almost afraid that the radiance of the Royal presence would dazzle her.

What happened next came as a horrible shock to Frances. She heard the sound of a loud slap, followed by a muffled cry, and then a shrill, angry voice shouted, 'So you'll defy me, will you, Mistress? I'll have none of your impudence at *my* Court! You'll learn modesty and decorum, you baggage, or I'll pack you home to your father's house and never allow you into my presence again.' The shrill voice followed up this threat with an obscene oath which Master Fernandez did not allow his children to use, though they occasionally heard it on the lips of market traders.

Frances trembled, for she felt she knew the owner of the

voice. Summoning up all her courage she peeped through the gap in the hedge and saw what she had feared to see – the Queen scolding an unfortunate maid of honour, who was quietly weeping into a tiny lace-edged handkerchief.

'Answer me, you saucy minx!' screamed Elizabeth. 'Do you deny that you were flirting with young Sidney? Do you deny it?'

But the girl obviously did not dare reply, or even cry loudly, for she seemed to be choking back her tears as best as she could.

A few moments earlier, Frances had felt she could not believe her ears. Now, seeing the Queen only a few inches away, she could not believe her eyes. The afternoon sun glared down cruelly on Elizabeth's face, showing up every furrow and wrinkle in the skin that had looked as smooth as marble by torchlight and candlelight. Frances saw now that the face was heavily daubed with powder and rouge; that the neck rising so gracefully from the huge pearl-embroidered ruff was as scraggy as a hen's, and that several of the Royal teeth were missing. Worst of all, an angry frown sat where the radiant smile had been. Frances shuddered, and felt sick.

Why, she's not a goddess at all . . . she's just a bad-tempered old woman, she thought. How can I possibly plead with *her* for poor Dr Lopez's life? She would send me to the Tower as soon as I opened my mouth. No, I can't . . . I must run away before she finds me.

This time, however, escape was not so easy. Frances had intended to creep along behind the hedge until she was well out of Elizabeth's sight and hearing. Unfortunately, her toe stubbed against a loose piece of gravel and she fell forward, grabbing at the hedge to steady herself. But the twigs snapped in her fingers, and she went crashing through the gap, falling in a breathless heap right at the feet of the Queen and her maid of honour.

Frances shut her eyes in terror, imagining the two women

staring at her. Then she heard the Queen's voice – it sounded astonished now, rather than angry – saying, 'Who in God's name is this? Do I have spies lurking behind every hedge in my garden?' and the maid of honour replying, 'It looks like one of the pages, Madam.'

'Nonsense, I am well acquainted with all my pages,' snapped Elizabeth. 'I know who this is – he is one of the choristers who took part in the masque today. *I* recognize the livery, even if *you* do not, Mistress Arabella. Stand up, boy. What is your name, and what do you want of us?'

Now that the time had come, Frances could think of nothing more original to say than, 'May it please Your Majesty, I crave a boon.' But scarcely had she said it than a sudden faintness came over her, and she felt as if she were plunging into a dark well.

She emerged from the darkness to find someone shaking her shoulder and saying, not unkindly, 'Come, rouse yourself, young mistress. Have my stewards not been feeding you properly, that you collapse at my feet?'

Frances stared up, aghast, into the Queen's face, and thought she saw a twinkle in those keen, blue-shadowed eyes, though she could not be altogether sure.

'But . . . but, how did Your Majesty guess . . .?' she stammered, and Elizabeth laughed outright.

'How did I guess you were a girl in disguise? Why, it is easy, for *me* . . . I have learned to read faces. I can look at a minister and tell if he is wise; I can look at a courtier and tell if he is loyal . . . and do you think I cannot tell a girl from a boy? But I need you to tell me how this came about. Speak . . . what are you doing in doublet and hose when you should be wearing a petticoat?'

Frances began to tell her story, stammering at first, but encouraged by the look of growing kindness on the Queen's face. She described Thomas Mendes, and told how she dreaded the thought of marrying him, and how she had longed to have just one adventure before entering upon the dull business of being an adult and a wife. As she spoke, she saw Elizabeth's face soften once more into the smile that had dazzled her in the long gallery, and Mistress Arabella's face relax in relief that *she* was no longer the object of the Queen's interest.

'You are a wench of spirit . . . I wish I had some like you at my Court,' said Elizabeth when Frances had finished. 'I think I am the only woman in this realm who cannot be given in marriage against her will, and for that I suppose I should be grateful. But now let us speak of this favour that you would ask of me . . .'

Frances's heart sank. Faced with so much Royal kindness, she had almost forgotten her reason for waylaying the Queen. But before she could speak, Elizabeth added, 'I think I can guess at it. You hoped that I might intercede with your father and command him to set you free from this marriage contract. But alas, child, I have no power to do so. I may arrange marriages for my courtiers and maids of honour, or forbid them to wed – and rebuke them, too, when their behaviour merits it (and here the Queen turned to glare at Mistress Arabella, who blushed a deep crimson), but I have no authority over the private lives of my common subjects. You must marry the man your father has chosen, and I can do nothing to prevent it.'

'If it please Your Majesty,' replied Frances, surprised to find that her voice had turned to a croak, 'that is not the favour I came to ask.'

'Then what do you want of us? Speak up, child . . . clear your throat if you must.'

Frances prostrated herself at the Queen's feet, feeling the gravel path rough against her forehead.

'Your Majesty,' she said, and her voice was steady now, 'please spare the life of Dr Rodrigo Lopez. He is a loyal subject, and loves you better than anything else in this world.'

There was a long silence, a silence so profound that Frances could hear grasshoppers chirping in the shadow of the hedge. She raised her eyes and stared at the Queen's hands, and it seemed to her that the knuckles had tightened. Elizabeth's hands, unlike her face, looked smooth and white even in the glare of the afternoon sun. They were covered with rings, and Frances wondered if one of them might be the ruby ring which Dr Lopez had presented to his gracious mistress in happier times. But there were at least half a dozen rubies on the Queen's fingers, so it was impossible to tell.

'Are you a relative of Dr Lopez?' asked Elizabeth at last.

'Oh no, Your Majesty,' replied Frances quickly, feeling that she had already said too much. 'I am a good Christian, and come from an old Christian family. But Dr Lopez is a good friend to my father.' Then she looked up, and was astonished by the look of sadness on the Queen's face.

'It is hard for you to understand, child,' said Elizabeth, and her voice was not only sad but somehow profoundly weary. 'You look at me and think I am power personified, that no one in all this realm is more powerful. You think I have only to raise my little finger and empires will crumble, ships sail out across unknown seas, armies march into war, and men become ennobled or lay their heads on the block. Well, that is true enough. I am the Queen, and power is vested in me. But I am Queen only through the love of my people, and I can continue to reign only so long as I have their love. Do you understand what that means?' Frances shook her head, and Elizabeth went on: 'It means that I sometimes have to do things that make me shudder when I think of them. It means that I must please my people, even if by doing so I cannot please myself. And my people are not yet ready to accept Jews and foreigners as their equals and fellows.'

138

'But Dr Lopez is innocent,' cried Frances desperately. 'He has never worked except for Your Majesty's good.'

'That may be so,' replied the Queen with a sigh, 'but I know nothing of it. I only know what my ministers have advised me. They are wise men, all of them, and I put my trust in their judgement. But now I must return to the dancing, or my guests will think I am neglecting them. I am pleased with you, child, even though I cannot grant your request. You have courage, and that is a rare quality.' She held out her hand, and Frances kissed it gingerly, feeling the Royal rings hard and cold against her lips.

The Queen turned away, followed by the silent Mistress Arabella, leaving Frances with her head full of tangled thoughts. She could not understand all that Elizabeth had been trying to tell her; she only understood that there could be no reprieve for Dr Lopez. Sad and perplexed, she watched as the Queen began to walk in the direction of the Palace. She watched until, outlined against the horizon, the tired old woman with the heavily powdered face had turned once more into a golden goddess in whom all power was personified.

Chapter Eleven

On a sunny morning in June 1594, Dr Rodrigo Lopez, one-time chief physician to the Queen, was hanged for High Treason. Bound to a hurdle, which was drawn at the tail of a cart, he was dragged past his house in Holborn, past his orchard and his treasured herb garden, and West along the road to Tyburn, where the dreadful gallows stood.

The day had been proclaimed a holiday, since the three men who were being executed (Signor Ferreira and Signor Tinoco were to be hanged along with Dr Lopez) had all been found guilty of plotting against the Queen's life. Since the crack of dawn the townsfolk had been making for Tyburn, most of them carrying flagons of ale and baskets containing their dinners, many in their best clothes, some singing bawdy songs, and all of them laughing and jostling each other and in the highest of spirits.

'Such things are better than a play or a bear-baiting,' said

Father bitterly, as a group of revellers came ambling past the Fernandez house, filling the air with their strident mirth. 'I think we – we and the rest of our community – must be the only folk in London who are not on their way to see the fun.'

Robin shivered, remembering how Dr Lopez had once said to him, 'These gallants who write exquisite poetry would come to see you or me hanged at Tyburn without losing any of their appetite for dinner.' He had not completely understood the doctor's words then, but he understood them now.

The Fernandez family were exhausted, for they had not been to bed all night, but had spent the long hours praying that Dr Lopez might face his terrible death with courage, and that his soul might find peace in Heaven. Now, as the red light of dawn spilled over the pointed rooftops, they gathered bleary-eyed in the small dining-parlour and tried to eat their breakfast. But no one could swallow a morsel, and they soon gave up trying, and sat bleakly staring at each other across the table.

The hour set for the execution was approaching fast, and each person had his or her private vision of that horror. Soon, very soon, thought Robin, the cart carrying Dr Lopez would reach Tyburn, and the frightened old man would catch his first glimpse of the jeering crowd of spectators, the gallows, and the black-masked executioner with his grisly implements of death. Robin shut his eyes, but the picture in his mind remained as clear as ever. His hands were frozen, even though it seemed the day was going to be hot, and he tried in vain to warm them inside his doublet.

At last Mother broke the silence.

'It would not have been *quite* so bad,' she said with a sob, 'if the poor doctor had been beheaded on Tower Hill like a gentleman, instead of being hanged at Tyburn as if he were any common criminal. The disgrace of it . . . to be strung up on the same gallows as highway robbers and petty thieves . . . he, who was the Queen's private physician . . .'

'Be quiet, you silly woman,' shouted Father, his gloom turned to sudden anger. 'Is that all that troubles you? The manner of the good doctor's death is the least of our misfortunes. Has it not occurred to you that this may lead to a new wave of Jew-baiting? We shall have to lie low and scarcely breathe for the next few months . . . we may even be obliged to go back to Bristol. And poor Mistress Lopez . . . have you not thought of how she is going to suffer? Oh, I am not speaking now of the loss of her husband, though that is painful enough. But she will also be disgraced and destitute . . . her home and all her fortune taken from her, and only her father's charity to keep her from starvation.'

The children stared at Father, their mouths wide open in astonishment. Then Robin stammered, 'But what do you mean, sir? Why should Mistress Lopez be made destitute?'

Father sighed.

'You children were born in this country,' he said, 'and yet you know little enough about its laws and customs. Have you never heard that when a man is convicted of High Treason, as Dr Lopez was, all his lands and possessions and money . . . indeed, everything he owns . . . are forfeit to the Crown?'

A chill came over Robin. Here was something new . . . something he had never dreamed of. The vision of Dr Lopez mounting the scaffold faded from his mind, and instead he saw Mistress Lopez, her few personal belongings on her back, driven from the fine house that had been her home, and wandering, a fugitive, across the fields of Holborn.

As Robin and Philip passed through Paul's Churchyard next morning on the way to school, they saw a huge and excited crowd milling about a particular bookstall which seemed to be selling nothing but printed pamphlets. A little breeze had

142

sprung up and was blowing them about, and one of them, stained with mud from the cobblestones, wrapped itself around Robin's foot. He picked it up. A drawing confronted him – three villainous-looking Spanish gentlemen, one with an exaggeratedly hooked nose, all dangling from a gallows, and, underneath, a set of doggerel verses describing the execution in clumsy rhyme.

Robin showed it to Philip, who shuddered.

'These pamphleteers haven't lost any time,' said Robin, trying to sound nonchalant. 'But their work isn't worth a halfpenny.' And he deliberately dropped the pamphlet and trampled it back in the mud.

When the boys arrived at school, more of the vile drawings greeted them. All their classmates seemed to be reading these pamphlets or others like them as they waited for Master Breakstaff to arrive, and the shrill and excited talk was all of the execution.

'You should have been there – you missed the most splendid treat,' said Richard Lucy happily as soon as he espied Robin. '*Everyone* was there, even young Courtney, and he's as big a milksop as you are. You enjoyed it, didn't you, Courtney?' And Richard playfully punched young Courtney, who squirmed without much apparent pleasure.

'I don't know how you can watch people being killed,' said Robin, imagining he could see a flicker of fellow feeling on Courtney's face. But he knew he must keep anger out of his voice. He had kept his own Marrano connections secret until now. On no account must he appear sympathetic towards Lopez, the traitor.

'But these people *deserved* punishment – they had plotted to kill our Lady the Queen,' protested Richard. 'By going to see them hanged we were only showing ourselves to be loyal citizens.'

'Fine words,' retorted Robin bitterly. 'You know well

143

enough that you go to executions because you enjoy them. No bear-baiting was ever so exciting.'

'You might well have said that if you had been at Tyburn yesterday,' broke in a tall boy named Nicholas Riley. 'Oh, it started off quite tamely . . . the old Jew was certainly no hero. He looked like a frightened little old ferret up there on the scaffold, and he made a speech that was very funny. Do you know what the old Jew said? He actually declared that he loved his mistress the Queen better than he loved Jesus Christ! Of course, everyone laughed at that.' Hearing the story repeated, all the boys laughed again.

Out of the corner of his eyes Robin saw Philip turning green. Luckily the other boys were so engrossed in the previous day's adventures that nobody noticed.

'You haven't told him the most exciting part,' interrupted Richard, his eyes shining. Then, turning to Robin, he went on. 'The hangman disposed of the old Jew and one of the Spaniards quite quickly, and then it was the turn of the other Spaniard . . . Tinoco, I think his name was. Well, he was a fine young fellow, not a whey-faced coward like the other two, for he fell upon the executioner, and tried to kill him. I've been to dozens of executions, but this was the first time I've known anything like this happen. Yes, he took on the hangman in single combat, and they wrestled with each other for a long time, and lots of people in the crowd cheered him on, for all that he was an enemy of the Queen. Everyone admires courage.'

'But of course he couldn't win,' Nicholas broke in. 'Some fine fellows in the crowd saw that he was getting the better of the hangman, and they jumped on him and overpowered him, and so he was brought to the gallows at last. And good riddance too. We can do without foreigners and Jews in the Queen's realm.'

Robin thought for a moment, and then summoned up all his courage.

144

'But Dr Lopez wasn't really a Jew,' he said. 'He was baptized a Christian many years ago.'

'That means nothing,' said John Archer eagerly. 'I'll wager he was still practising his vile Jewish rites behind locked doors. They all do. My father says there are hundreds of New Christians in London who only *pretend* to keep the true faith but are still Jews in secret.'

'Yes, they poison wells and practise the black arts and crucify Christian children,' cried Richard. 'My father says we should send them all back and let the Inquisition deal with them.'

'If *I* were to meet a Jew,' said a big, powerfully-muscled boy named Henry Butler, 'I shouldn't wait for the Inquisition to deal with him. I should twist his neck myself, as if he were a roasting fowl.'

'All the more reason for you to get the Inquisition to roast him,' said Richard, and all the boys roared with laughter at this unexpected witticism.

Robin suddenly took his courage and his life in both hands.

'If you were to discover that *I* were a Jew,' he asked, 'would you hand *me* over to the Inquisition?'

Philip's mouth fell open in dismay. Robin saw, through a kind of haze, the other boys staring at him. What have I done? he thought. What have I done?

'What are you saying? *Are* you a Jew?' asked Richard at last.

'Of course not,' replied Robin quickly. 'We have always been good Christians. I was only testing your friendship. If I were a Jew, would you truly give me up to be tortured and burned?'

'If you were a Jew you could not be my friend,' said Richard. 'There are you answered?'

The sudden arrival of Master Breakstaff, full of wrath at the abysmal standard of the Latin exercises he had just been correcting, brought the discussions to a close. But for the

145

rest of the morning, even as he struggled with Caesar's Gallic Wars and felt the schoolmaster's cane biting into his back, Robin had a new worry to contend with. He knew now that, if the worst were to happen, he could expect no mercy from Richard Lucy, his best friend.

Chapter Twelve

In the end it was not Richard who proved disloyal, but one of the neighbours. Master Sadler, who knew well enough that the Fernandez family were New Christians, had always seemed friendly. But after Dr Lopez's execution, his friendship cooled. A stone shattered a window in the Fernandez house next day, and the boys came home from school to find a gallows cartoon grinning at them from the lintel.

'It must have been Master Sadler,' said Mother tearfully. 'He called after me this morning when I went out to visit Mistress Mendes. I had scarce put my head out of doors when he shouted, "Away with you, foul Jewess! We shall soon be rid of all you poisoners and traitors!"'

'We must leave London,' declared Father. 'I had hoped it might not come to this.'

'Are we running away?' asked Robin, aghast, seeing himself a fugitive like Anthony Lopez.

'I trust we need not run; we still have a coach and sturdy horses,' said father with a wry smile. 'Some of our friends are going abroad; Master Ames, I know, plans to follow his grandson to Antwerp. But I have no wish to leave England. We shall go to Bristol to stay with Uncle Ruy until this cruel time is past.'

Mother seemed to be expecting this news. 'The Mendes family are going to Amsterdam,' she said. 'Mistress Mendes has a sister living there.'

'Are they taking Thomas with them?' asked Frances eagerly.

'They would scarcely leave him here. Mistress Mendes tells me they hope to stay in Amsterdam, so I fear you have lost your husband, Frances.'

If Mother had thought her daughter would be sorry to hear this news, she was soon disillusioned. Frances clapped her hands and danced so jubilantly that Mother threatened to thrash her. But while Robin was pleased that Frances had been released from the dreary Thomas, he could not share her elation. He could only think that the family was leaving London, city of wondrous delights, and that although its sweets had unexpectedly turned sour, Bristol would be a very dull place by comparison.

Dunstan Ames called on the Fernandez family a few days later, to make his farewells before leaving for Antwerp.

'London is not a city where a Jew can live now, not even in secret,' he sighed, as he slumped wearily in a chair and accepted a tankard of mead from Mother. 'I had hoped this affair might be forgotten as soon as my poor son-in-law was despatched, but the populace seems set on remembering. Did you know that a vile fellow named Thomas Nashe has just published a scurrilous book about two Jewish poisoners? They call it *The Unfortunate Traveller*. One of the Jews is presented as the Pope's physician. It is not hard to guess who

148

was the model for *that*! Down in Paul's Churchyard it is selling as fast as hot pies. If I had my way, all ballad-mongers and play-makers would be whipped through the town.' Here Master Ames looked accusingly at Robin, who could not help feeling guilty.

'Surely Master Shakespeare is not evil, sir,' he ventured at last.

'They are all as bad as each other,' snapped Master Ames. 'Did you know that another of these villains has had an antisemitic play performed at the Rose Theatre? They call it *The Jew of Malta*; the man who wrote it is one Christopher Marlowe . . . a plague on him! I thought it my duty to see it, and now I cannot get the wretched thing out of my head. The play ended with a horrible greedy Jew called Barabas being boiled to death in a cauldron that he had prepared for someone else. And then the worst thing happened . . .' Here Master Ames paused, and mopped his sweating brow.

'What could be worse than a boiling cauldron?' asked Mother curiously.

'As he writhed in the steam, confessing his many sins and cursing his enemies, the audience cheered and jeered, and then began to shout his name. The name was not Barabas. It was Lopez.'

A flood of horror swept over Robin. In his mind's eye he saw the wondrous theatre, and the glittering costumes, and the silken flag hanging on the sky, and he heard the audience chanting his old friend's name. He was scarcely aware that Dunstan Ames was still speaking.

'Yes, I am glad to be leaving for a more hospitable shore,' he went on. 'And I am thankful that Anthony is safe in Antwerp. His mother received a letter from him yesterday by a trusted messenger – a merchant colleague of my brother, now visiting London on business. The letter assures her that the boy is well and happy.'

149

'No doubt Mistress Lopez will soon join him in Antwerp,' said Mother.

'In Antwerp? No, not she. My daughter is not going with me. She has chosen to remain here.'

'But where will she live?'

'Why in Holborn, of course. She says she wishes to remain in the house where she and her husband were happy together.'

'But I thought . . .' Father began, and then broke off, wondering how to express himself tactfully.

'You thought the property of convicted traitors was forfeit to the Crown,' replied Master Ames. 'Certainly that is the law. But the Queen has been merciful. Soon after my son-in-law died, she sent a messenger to inform Catherine that she might retain his house, his fortune and his property.'

'That is most generous of her,' said Father, impressed.

Master Ames smiled wryly.

'Is that all it means to you, Master Fernandez?' he asked.

'What more *can* it mean?'

'Well, let me tell you something more. Dr Nunez came to see me last week. He is, as you know, still a frequent visitor at Court, and is often privileged to be in the presence of the Queen. He told me that Her Majesty still wears the ruby ring my son-in-law gave her. A convicted traitor, and yet she still wears his ring. Well, do you still not understand?'

The Fernandez family looked at him, not daring to put their thoughts into words.

'She has refused to take possession of my son-in-law's property,' Master Ames went on, 'and she still wears his ring. There is only one thing it can possibly mean. *She never believed him guilty.*'

The family was packing the last of its belongings before leaving for Bristol when an unexpected visitor arrived.

All the house was in turmoil – not the happy turmoil that

usually preceded festivals, but something more disturbing. Everything of value that could be carried, from household utensils to money, jewellery and clothes, was being packed in chests and piled into a waiting cart. It was no different from their move from Bristol to London, thought Robin, yet somehow it was much harder. That last time they had come seeking adventure; this time they were going as refugees, driven away by ignorance and fear.

It was amidst the scurrying servants and the scattered possessions that the visitor appeared. Master Shakespeare stood in the doorway, looking on the scene with puzzled eyes.

'But why are you leaving London?' he cried. 'I had thought you were staying with us for good, Master Fernandez.'

'For good, not ill, Master Shakespeare,' replied Father grimly. 'A great misfortune has fallen upon us, as you may have heard. We are going back to Bristol, and I pray God we have no need to travel further.'

Will Shakespeare sat down on an upturned chest, and shook his head sadly.

'I did not know,' he said at last. 'I had come to enquire why you have not been at the rehearsals for our new play, Robin. I thought you might be sick.'

'We are all sick . . . sick and reviled,' interrupted Father. 'My son will not perform in your theatre again, Master Shakespeare. We have had enough of plays and players. We heard about *The Jew of Malta*. We know how the audience shouted "Lopez! Lopez!" while the Jew died in torment.'

'Of course it was hard on you, seeing that you knew the man,' replied Will Shakespeare thoughtfully, reaching out for the tankard of wine that Mother had brought.

Robin felt a sudden unease. At first he had been glad to see Will Shakespeare, as lively and warm with friendship as ever. But now it seemed to him that Master Shakespeare was too little concerned about Dr Lopez's death.

151

'He was a good man,' Robin broke in. 'His only care in life was to heal the sick. So why do they all hate him? Why did my Lord Essex hate him?'

'Oh, my Lord Essex didn't hate him,' replied Master Shakespeare, and the Fernandez family looked at him in astonishment.

'But he worked against him,' said Father.

'Ah yes, I'll grant that he worked against him, but that wasn't through hate. You see, I know the whole story. My Lord Essex is my friend, and he told me everything.'

'Then why? Why did he do it?'

'Lord Essex didn't hate your Dr Lopez. He just had to be proved right. As soon as he suspected that the good doctor might be in some way involved with Spain, he took his suspicions to the Queen. But instead of listening to him with courtesy, Her Majesty sent him away with a flea in his ear. She said he was a rash, temerarious youth, and that Dr Lopez was undoubtedly innocent. A man like Essex cannot endure insults. From that moment on, he swore he would be proved right.'

A feeling of cold horror came over Robin. In his mind's eye he saw the tall, handsome figure of Lord Essex standing in the blazing vestibule of his home, his face glowing with kindness, bidding his guests welcome. And then in its place came another picture . . . a little old man feebly climbing the steps of a scaffold.

'And if he hadn't been proved right,' he asked, 'would it have mattered?'

'It would have mattered to Essex.'

'But how can you tell us this so calmly? You yourself once said that a poor beetle suffers as much when you tread on it as a giant suffers when he dies. Dr Lopez was a giant, and yet you pity him less than if he had been a beetle.'

Will Shakespeare looked at Robin with interest.

'Did I really say that?' he asked.

'Yes, you did.'

'It's a good line – I must use it in a play some time. Thank you for reminding me.'

For the first time since he had known him, Robin felt angry with Master Shakespeare. He forgot that his family were staring at him open-mouthed, and that a well-brought-up boy did not argue with adults.

'All you care for is your theatre, sir,' he said bitterly, 'and yet it breeds hatred against us. The villain of Marlowe's play was a Jew, and he was a hideous monster.'

'Come, Robin, you know that every play must have a villain, unless it be a love story. A play without a villain would be a dull piece indeed. If I were to write a play about a good man who does nothing but say his prayers and give alms to the poor, the audience would cut my throat – and ask for its money back afterwards.'

'But why must the Jew be the villain? Why can't he be the hero?' persisted Robin.

Will Shakespeare smiled, and patted his shoulder.

'No audience would accept such a thing,' he said. 'The time has not yet come.'

'Then if we can't be heroes, why can't we at least be human beings? *You* know we don't hate Christians, or poison wells, or gloat over our money-bags. You know we're just people like any other, except that we live in fear of our lives. Such inventions do us nothing but harm. You won't let us be giants, but why do we have to be horned beasts?'

There was a long silence. Then Will Shakespeare, with his eyes cast down, replied, 'You are right, I cannot deny it. I must leave you now, my good friends . . . I am summoned to a rehearsal. God speed you on your way and care for you until we meet again.' And with a quick handshake for Mother and Father, and another pat on the shoulder for the children, Master Shakespeare was gone.

153

'He left in a hurry,' said Father, smiling bitterly. 'These are your friends, Robin. I am glad you spoke up as you did.'

Robin could not reply; he was too torn by conflicting emotions . . . astonishment that Father should have admired his impudence instead of thrashing him, and fear that he might have offended his friend.

He'll never come seeking me out again, he thought, that much is certain. Even if we ever return to London, I'll not see him any more.

If Robin could have seen Will Shakespeare later that day, he would have been surprised. The playwright was seated at his writing table, a manuscript spread before him. For a while he hesitated over it, flicking through the sheaf of papers. Then, with a sigh, he pitched it in the grate, set light to it, and watched it shrivel to ashes.

Chapter Thirteen

A year went by before Robin met Will Shakespeare again.

The family had returned from Bristol, now that the wave of anti Jewish feeling that had followed Dr Lopez's execution had subsided. Robin was fourteen now, and was apprenticed to the Grocers' Guild. Philip was still at school, but took no more part in theatricals. Frances was the happiest of the three Fernandez children, for there was talk of a marriage between her and Anthony Lopez, now that dreary Thomas was safely despatched to Amsterdam. Anthony was home again with his mother, his hopes of a career at Court dashed, but willing enough to become a merchant grocer like his grandfather, and his future wife's family. Dunstan Ames had settled in Antwerp and was unlikely to return, and many other familiar faces were missing from the Marrano community, for Hector Nunez and several other people had stopped attending synagogue services.

Sometimes as Robin weighed out sugar and spices in his master's dim warehouse, or entered accounts in the ledger, or swept the floors, or took down the shutters, or played at football with the other apprentices, he found himself wondering whether all the marvels and terrors of the previous year – the masques and theatres and great houses, the feasts and conspiracies, the summons to Whitehall Palace and the execution of Dr Lopez – had really happened at all, or whether they were simply visions born of his own imagination.

He was walking along London Bridge one morning, on his way to deliver a letter from his master to a haberdasher who had his shop there, when somebody called his name. It was with mixed feelings that he recognized Will Shakespeare. But Master Shakespeare seemed to bear no grudges. His smile was as warm and his hug as affectionate as ever, and the familiar odour of new parchment and old ale still clung about him, bringing back memories of livelier times.

'And so you are a slave to some fusty grocer now, are you?' he asked, after he had invited Robin to take a cup of ale with him and Robin had regretfully declined. 'Is he such a tyrant, this master of yours?'

'Oh no, sir, but his time is money, and he does not allow me to waste it.'

'Ah yes, I know the type. I was apprenticed to a glover – a friend of my father. He was a kind enough man; he didn't starve me and he beat me only once a day. But he would not allow me any free time to see the strolling players when they came to Stratford. Such treatment was more than I could bear, of course, so I left off making gloves and became an actor, much to my father's disgust.'

Robin smiled wistfully.

'Oh, *I* shall not leave my master,' he said. 'One day I shall be a master grocer myself, and have sacks of cinnamon and apprentices of my own. The stage is not for me.'

'Yes,' replied Master Shakespeare with a little sigh, 'you made that plain the last time we met.'

'The last time we met I was rude to you,' broke in Robin quickly. 'I apologize for that, sir. It has been on my conscience all this past year.'

'Rude? No, indeed, I am thankful for it. You did me a great service.'

'I . . . I don't understand, sir,' faltered Robin.

'At that time I was writing a new play,' Master Shakespeare replied. 'The leading character was a Jew named Shylock, and I regret to say that he was a blood-brother to Kit Marlowe's Barabas. A horned beast, as you would call him . . . a monster to be hissed and hated. I knew no better, you see, until you opened my eyes.'

'*I* opened your eyes?'

'Of course. It was the sufferings that Master Marlowe's play inflicted on you. Indeed, I could not bear it. You taught me that Jews are human beings, to be presented as such on the stage. And so, after leaving you, I went home and burned my play. I have rewritten it, and more to your taste, I think. No, there is no need to look so happy. I could not make the Jew a hero . . . such a thing would not be allowed . . . no audience would accept it. He is still the villain of the piece, but a human villain, I think. He may not be a giant, but at least he is less of a horned beast.'

'I wish I could see that play,' said Robin regretfully.

Will Shakespeare laughed, and patted his shoulder.

'I had been planning to visit your father,' he said. 'My play is called *The Merchant of Venice* – it opens at the Rose on the fourteenth of this month. How if I appealed to your father to intercede with your master and ask if you might have special leave from work to see the play?'

'I . . . I should like that indeed, sir.'

'Good, I shall do it this afternoon, and I do not see how they can refuse. After all, in a sense, it is your play.'

★   ★   ★

So here he was once again in the theatre, watching the rest of the audience arrive, sniffing the splendid theatre smell of sawdust and grease-paint and orange peel, and hearing the musicians tuning their instruments in their gallery below the Heavens.

The trumpets sounded and the play began, and soon Master Burbage strode on to the stage in the role of Shylock, the Jew of Venice. A storm of cheers, jeers and catcalls greeted him. He could have been the twin brother to Marlowe's Barabas. The fusty robes were the same; so were the tangled locks and flowing beard, and one could almost see the Devil's horns curling under his yellow cap. Yet Master Shakespeare had promised . . . Robin leaned forward and gripped the edge of his bench with sweating hands, his heart pounding with excitement and fear.

Certainly this Shylock could not be called a good man. Like Barabas, he loved his money and hated the Christians of the city; indeed, he even plotted to destroy a certain merchant whose name was Antonio. And yet he was not altogether evil; he loved his daughter and his dead wife and his religion, and there was something dignified about him. The audience, which had begun by hissing and jeering at his every utterance, soon grew quiet, and there was even a murmur of approval when he said:

> 'For sufferance is the badge of all our tribe;
> You call me misbeliever, cut-throat dog,
> And spit upon my Jewish gaberdine,
> And all for use of that which is mine own.
> Well then, it now appears you need my help . . .'

Why, this is very different from Kit Marlowe's play, thought Robin. At least Shylock is a real person with real grievances, not some make-believe monster who hates for the sake of hating. I should still like to see Master Shakespeare

158

write a play with a Jew as a hero, but I know that cannot be. Not in our time. In the time to come, God willing . . .

The play progressed, and so did Shylock's evil intentions, and yet he retained his humanity. Then came a scene in which the Jew was being baited by two young fops, and suddenly Robin sat bolt upright, for Shylock was speaking these words:

'If you prick us, do we not bleed? If you tickle us, do we not laugh? If you poison us, do we not die? And if you wrong us, shall we not revenge?'

A feeling of great gladness and comfort came over Robin, for in that moment he knew how the words would ring down the centuries, and that the time would come when St Olave's children would no longer be horned beasts, but even giants, perhaps.

Epilogue

The time did come, and Robin lived to see it. In 1656, as the result of a petition presented to Oliver Cromwell by Rabbi Manasseh ben Israel, of Amsterdam, the Jews in England were at last given permission to practise their religion openly. They have done so ever since.

In 1702, the former Marrano community consecrated a magnificent synagogue in Bevis Marks, not far from St Olave's, Hart Street. Their descendants still worship there today.